Praise for

NIGHT ON FIRE

"The novel takes readers on an aching journey of self-discovery at a time when figuring out the world meant facing devastating truths about where you lived and what you loved...Kidd writes with insight and restraint, creating a richly layered opus that hits every note to perfection...Billie's coming of age could serve as a cautionary tale about where America once was and why we all need to stay vigilant, lest we return—as current headlines attest. Beautifully written and earnestly delivered, the novel rolls to an inexorable, stunning conclusion readers won't soon forget."
—*Kirkus Reviews* starred review

"Billie comes to grips with her own prejudices...in a way that is both lyrical and honest. In a year in which news events have made it clear that the Civil Rights Movement is far from over, titles like Kidd's have special resonance...Billie's internal thoughts about the two Annistons—the one she knows, and the one Jermaine knows—seem in many ways a mirror to the present...Moving, powerful, and deeply relevant today."—*Booklist* starred review

NIGHT ON FIRE

RONALD KIDD

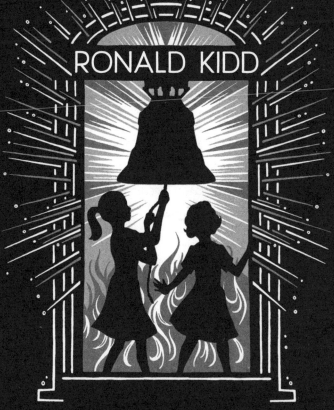

ALBERT WHITMAN & COMPANY
CHICAGO, ILLINOIS

To Ida Sue Kidd,
who taught me what was right

Library of Congress Cataloging-in-Publication data
Names: Kidd, Ronald.
Title: Night on fire / Ronald Kidd.
Description: Chicago, Illinois : Albert Whitman & Company, 2015. | Summary:
"When thirteen-year-old Billie Sims learns that the Freedom Riders, a civil rights
group protesting segregation on buses in the summer of 1961, will be traveling
through Anniston, Alabama, she thinks change could be coming to her stubborn town.
But what starts as angry grumbles soon turns to brutality, and Billie is forced to
reconsider her own views"—Provided by publisher.
Identifiers: LCCN 2015025153 | ISBN 9780807570265
Subjects: | CYAC: Civil rights movements—Fiction. | Segregation—Fiction. | Race
relations—Fiction. | African Americans—Fiction. | Anniston (Ala.)— History—
20th century—Fiction. | Alabama—History—20th century—Fiction.
Classification: LCC PZ7.K5315 Ni 2015 | DDC [Fic]—dc23
LC record available at http://lccn.loc.gov/2015025153

Article on vii from the *Montgomery Advertiser*.
Articles on 71, 108, 126, and 256 from the *Anniston Star*.

Printed in the United States of America
10 9 8 7 6 5 4 3 2 1 BP 20 19 18 17 16

Design by Jordan Kost
Cover image © David Wardle

For more information about Albert Whitman & Company,
visit our web site at www.albertwhitman.com.

WASHINGTON (AP) – Thirteen bus riders—six white, seven Negro—left Thursday on a 13-day journey to challenge racial segregation in the Deep South. They promise they'll go to jail if necessary.

The group plans to protest separate restaurant, washroom and other facilities for whites and Negroes at bus terminals and rest-stops.

"We shall not be moved," they softly sang to the tune of an old Negro spiritual as they boarded two regularly scheduled buses.

The trip is sponsored by the Congress of Racial Equality (CORE).

The riders plan to wind up May 17 at New Orleans after stops at Richmond; Petersburg and Lynchburg, Va.; Greensboro and Charlotte N.C.; Rock Hill and Sumter, S.C.; Augusta and Atlanta, Ga.; Birmingham and Montgomery, Ala.; and Jackson, Miss.

The 13 plan to join a May 17 rally in New Orleans marking the seventh anniversary of the Supreme Court decision banning segregation in public schools.

Montgomery Advertiser, May 3, 1961

PROLOGUE

One day in the spring of 1961, my street was the center of the world.

People read about it in newspapers and watched it on TV. They heard about it on NBC, the BBC, and Radio Moscow. The president held meetings. The FBI investigated.

What they saw were Negroes and white people together—traveling, marching, getting beaten up and burned. It started in my little town of Anniston, Alabama, and it moved to Birmingham and Selma and Washington, DC. I watched the flames catch and spread to Montgomery, where they were fanned and blessed by Martin Luther King. The people sang, the mob roared, and I glimpsed freedom.

I thought freedom was just a word, but it's not. My friend Jarmaine taught me that. Freedom is hands and feet, bodies and faces, wounds and scars. It's a bell, and I rang it. It's a bus, and I climbed on. Along the way, I thought I would get answers. Instead, I found questions.

Why do people hate each other?

If a law is bad, should you break it?

How can good people be so cruel?

PART ONE
THE BUS

CHAPTER ONE

Let's get something straight. I'm not one of those gir-lie girls. I don't ooh and ahh. I don't giggle and blush. Dresses cramp my style. Petticoats make me itch.

Mama and Daddy wanted a boy named Billy. When I popped out, they shrugged and changed the *y* to *ie*. So I'm Billie—Billie Sims. I ride bikes and climb trees. I shoot off firecrackers. On Saturdays in the fall, Daddy and I throw the football and listen on the radio to John Forney, play-by-play announcer for the Alabama Crimson Tide.

One afternoon in May 1961, I sat cross-legged on my bed and gazed out the window. I checked my bus schedule, which was smudged and wrinkled from use. When I looked up, I caught a glimpse of my reflection in the glass. I'm thirteen, but I look older. Maybe it's because I'm tall. It could be my eyes, which according to my friend Grant say, *Don't mess with me.* My hair is what they call strawberry blond. I tie it back to keep it out of my face, but it always seems to come loose.

I glanced at the bus schedule and then at my watch. Folding up the schedule, I put it away, hopped off the bed, and went outside. Our house was at the top of a hill on the Birmingham Highway, about five miles west of town. It was a white bungalow with a wide porch and a hedge along the front. Next door was a home built with river stones, and its tan, lumpy walls reminded me of a gingerbread house.

In front, crouching by the steps, was my best friend, Grant McCall. Grant was a month older than I was and thought it gave him the right to boss me around. You'd think he would know better by now. Grant was a little taller than me, with black hair that stuck up in back. He had a long, friendly face, when you could see it. Most of the time it was covered up by his camera, which was as much a part of his body as his nose or eyes.

Grant had moved next door with his mom and dad a few years back, when Mr. McCall had been hired as the lead reporter at the *Anniston Star*, our local newspaper. They had come from Cincinnati, where Mr. McCall had worked on a big paper with lots of reporters. Grant said his father had been looking for a small town with a good paper, a place where he could make a difference, and had found it in Anniston. Sometimes Mr. McCall's reporting made people mad, but they read it anyway, because even when they disagreed, they knew he would tell the truth. Once I asked him what he liked about Anniston.

"Important things are happening here," he'd said.

"Here?" I asked. "In Anniston?"

He smiled. "Open your eyes, Billie. Look around."

I headed across the yard toward Grant. I hadn't bothered to put on shoes, so the grass felt warm and dry beneath my feet. It was a sunny spring, and I'd been wearing shorts and a T-shirt for weeks.

"Hey!" I yelled.

Grant ignored me. He does that a lot. It's not that he's mean or anything. It's just that when he shoots photos, he's in his own little world, with a white border and glossy finish.

I tapped his shoulder. He juggled his camera, then stood up and wheeled around.

"Billie, how many times do I have to tell you—"

"I know, I know. 'Don't bother me when I'm taking pictures.' Well, you're always taking pictures. You might as well attach that camera to your head. Just graft it right on like a pear branch."

"Huh?"

I snapped my fingers in front of his face. "Hello! Can you hear me? There's a world out here."

"Look, I'm busy. What do you want?"

"It's Friday," I said.

"Just give me a minute, okay?"

"What are you taking pictures of?" I asked.

"Flowers. I'm trying out a new close-up lens."

"There's a special lens for close-ups?"

"There's a lens for everything," he said.

Grant snapped a few more pictures, then took the camera strap from around his neck, showed me the camera, and was off to the races, talking about his favorite topic. Blah blah blah *Minolta*. Blah blah blah *aperture*. Blah blah blah *telephoto*.

I noticed that he had a couple of freckles on his nose and a mole on one cheek. Do you call it a beauty mark if it's on a guy? A few beads of perspiration dotted his upper lip, and one of them dropped off as he spoke. His teeth were shiny and straight. His lips were soft. Okay, I didn't know that for sure.

"Well?" he said.

I shook my head. "Sorry, I didn't hear you."

"My new wide-angle lens. Do you want to see it?"

I said, "Of course."

He took off the close-up lens, then reached into his camera bag, pulled out a shorter lens, and clicked it into place.

"This one takes a wider picture," he said. "You know, for landscapes, things like that."

"Could I see?" I asked.

He handed me the camera. "Be careful. It's expensive."

I was surprised at how heavy it was. I thought of it almost as a toy, Grant's fancy toy. But it had weight and heft. Bringing it up to my eye, I looked through the lens and swiveled slowly around. Everything seemed far away, framed like a picture.

"Try looking over there," said Grant.

He touched my shoulders and turned me gently to the north, until I was gazing out over hills and trees. It looked like ordinary countryside, but I knew better.

"The army depot," I said.

The official name was the Anniston Ordnance Depot. It covered fifteen thousand acres, just down the hill from us. The people there serviced tanks and antiaircraft guns. At least one of them shuffled papers. I knew, because she was my mother.

I told Grant, "I want to take a picture. Could you show me how?"

"Just push the button," he said.

"Which one? How do I hold it?"

Grant rolled his eyes, then stepped behind me and guided my hands on the camera, my left hand supporting it and my right hand poised above the shutter button. I felt his breath on my cheek. It smelled like lemonade.

"Okay, push," he said.

There was a click, and the image blinked.

"Nothing to it," I said.

"That's the easy part. Now you have to develop the picture."

"Could you show me how?" I asked, leaning against him.

Grant stepped away, and I stumbled backward.

"Hey, watch it!" he said. "I told you, that's expensive."

He grabbed the camera and cradled it in his arms the way you might hold a puppy, or a girl if you had a clue.

I looked at my watch. "Come on, it's almost time. Let's go."

"Okay," he said, "but I'm bringing my camera."

* * *

"Here it comes!"

Grant pointed. I grinned and tied my hair back. On the horizon, beyond the trees and houses in my neighborhood, a speck appeared. It got bigger as we watched, moving along the road and up the hill. It formed a shape, fuzzy at first, then long and rounded, like one of the medicine capsules Mama took for her headaches. It disappeared behind some pine trees, then rounded a turn, and there it was.

It was a bus—not one of those beat-up city buses, but a gleaming Greyhound, with silver sides, a long blue stripe, windows that leaned forward, and five license plates, one for each state it went through.

"Now!" I yelled.

We pushed off from the hilltop and down the other side, pedaling like nobody's business. I owned a Schwinn, and Grant had a ten-speed racing bike, but to do this right, what we needed was gravity.

It was like a magic trick. I'd noticed it one day coming back from church with Mama and Daddy. Church wasn't Daddy's favorite place, so he tended to return home at high speed. He had pulled around to pass a car on the highway, and as we came up even with it, there was a moment when our speeds matched and our worlds clicked into place. In that instant, I could see their family as clearly as mine. The father frowned as he drove. The mother looked away and out the window. A little boy sat in back. He glanced at me and smiled. I was in another car, another world, but just for a second I was right there with him.

Grant and I had decided to try it with the bus. Sometimes it worked, and sometimes it didn't. We had to time it perfectly. If we left too soon, we would beat the bus to the bottom of the hill. If we started too late, the bus would drive by before we got going. But if we timed it just right, we got a ride to remember.

Picking up speed, Grant and I raced side by side down the two-lane highway, like the chariot drivers in *Ben-Hur*, a movie we'd watched at the Ritz Theater. Looking over our shoulders, we saw the bus reach the top of the hill and start down. It came up behind us and, little by little, pulled even. It was right next to us, huge, throwing off heat, tires whirring on the asphalt.

The wind whipped my hair. I gripped the handlebars, hard. Then suddenly, everything changed.

We were the ones standing still, and the highway sped by. Trees, houses, mailboxes flew past, racing up the hill. Meanwhile we were motionless, suspended in space, the bus floating alongside like a silver bubble. Bus passengers watched us through the windows. A little girl tugged her mother's sleeve. A man in a brown hat walked along the aisle, bracing himself on the seat backs.

I wondered where the passengers were going—Montgomery, Monroeville, Mobile. Miss Harper Lee lived in Monroeville. That very morning her picture had been in the paper, with an article saying she had won something called the Pulitzer Prize for *To Kill a Mockingbird*, a book she wrote. They said she had an apartment in New York City and lived in both places. I wished I could live in two places. I would live another life, an important life, doing things that mattered. I loved my family, but I wanted more. I didn't know what, but I needed it desperately, sometimes so much that it ached.

For a moment, I imagined what it would be like not just to chase the bus, but to get on it and leave. I'd travel to Montgomery, the capital of Alabama, or to Monroeville to visit Miss Harper Lee. Maybe she would take me to see her apartment in New York City. I could go anywhere and do whatever I wanted. I would be free.

Free. Mama said the word sometimes. Her eyes would light up and she'd gaze off into the distance. I wondered what she saw. Did it just mean getting away, like taking a trip? Maybe it was like summer vacation.

During school, the summer shimmered in the distance. Then it arrived with a rush, and classes were over. We could sleep late and roam the hills. We could do whatever we wanted, even if it just meant lying in the grass and watching the clouds. Is that what freedom was?

The bus edged forward, and the bubble burst. I was back on my bike, and the bus rumbled on. Grant and I skidded to a stop at the bottom of the hill, in front of Forsyth's Grocery. Grant lifted his camera and snapped some pictures of the bus as it disappeared down the highway.

Isn't it strange how things work? Soon Grant would take pictures again, but the bus wasn't driving along the highway. It was broken down by the road, sides battered, tires slashed. Glass shattered. People screamed. My rosy dreams gave way to a nightmare of blood and flames.

And it all happened on Mother's Day.

CHAPTER TWO

We dumped our bikes in front of Forsyth's Grocery and hurried inside, where it was cool and smelled like melons. Mr. Forsyth stood behind the counter, and his wife, Cleo, was busy arranging fruit in the produce section.

I called out, "Hey, Mrs. F. Save a kumquat for me."

A few customers wandered the aisles. Old Mrs. Todd was squeezing the bread. Bubba Jakes, a skinny kid in my class at school, was looking over safety razors, as if he needed one.

When we approached the counter, Mr. Forsyth shot us a tired grin. "So, kids, what'll it be?"

"The usual," I told him.

He reached under the counter, pulled out an open box of 45 rpm records, and set it in front of me.

"Have at it," he said.

The box contained the latest Top 40 hits, shipped in a batch every week so people like me could snap them up. I spent most of my allowance on records, and Daddy didn't like it.

"Paying for noise," he would grunt. "That's all you're doing."

At least it was better than Grant, who spent his allowance on bubble gum. Of course, it wasn't just any bubble gum, as he was quick to point out. It was Topps, and inside every package were baseball cards.

He bought five packages, the way he always did, ripped open the first, and thumbed through the cards inside.

"Frank Robinson!" he exclaimed, stuffing the gum into his mouth and chewing like a cow on caffeine.

Every week, Mr. Forsyth clipped a list of the Top 40 records from *Billboard Magazine* and taped it to the side of the box. Today the list showed that Elvis Presley had both the #2 and #3 records: "It's Now or Never" and "Are You Lonesome Tonight?" I elbowed Grant and showed him.

He snorted. "I can't believe you listen to that mush."

"It's not mush," I said. I had to admit though, I liked Elvis better when he was singing about jails and hound dogs.

Records cost more than bubble gum, so the most I could afford was one a week. I flipped through the box and found a song I had enjoyed on the radio.

Grant peered over my shoulder and burst out laughing. "'Itsy Bitsy Teenie Weenie Yellow Polka Dot Bikini'? I'd like to see you try one of those. You've got nothing to hold it up."

I felt my face get hot, but I didn't want him to know it. I ducked over to the cash register, reached into my pocket, and paid Mr. Forsyth.

"You kids are my best customers," he said. "Just spend more, huh?"

He gave me my change, then tore off a row of S&H Green Stamps and handed them to me. "Paste those in your coupon book. If you fill it up, you'll win something."

S&H Green Stamps were Mr. Forsyth's new scheme for promoting the store. You got some with every purchase, and if you filled enough coupon books, you could send off for a prize. He had planted an S&H sign out by the highway, where people would see it and come swarming in.

"Like bees to honey," he told me.

Or flies. Or mosquitoes. Or ants, like Grant and me.

Across the store, I spotted Janie, the youngest of the

Forsyth kids. She was twelve years old and a seventh grader at Wellborn Junior High. Janie had dark hair and glasses and usually could be found in a corner studying. Sometimes I thought she studied because it was the one thing that kept her parents from making her work in the store. But the studying must have paid off, because just a few weeks earlier Janie had won the Calhoun County spelling bee. Tomorrow she would go to Birmingham for the state bee, and half the neighborhood would be there to cheer her on.

I walked over and caught her eye. "Roll Tide," I said.

It was the state football cheer, but I thought it might be good for spelling too.

Janie flashed a shy grin. "Thanks, I guess."

"Ready for the big day?"

She showed me the book she was studying. It was a dictionary.

"Problem is, there are too many words," she said. "Darlene's been helping me though. I reckon I'll do all right."

Darlene was Janie's older sister. She had won the county spelling bee a few years before at age ten. Those Forsyth girls knew their alphabet. They were spelling fools.

"Janie?" said Grant, who had come up behind me.

She looked up, and Grant snapped her picture.

"Hey," she said, "I wasn't ready."

"That's the idea," said Grant. "It's candid. That means you don't pose. The picture shows what you're really like."

"So, what am I like?" asked Janie.

Grant gazed at her thoughtfully. "Smart. Nice."

There was a bump and a crash behind us, and Mr. Forsyth strode over toward the canned goods. We followed and saw a young Negro man about my age. I was surprised because we didn't usually see many Negroes in our neighborhood.

He was kneeling in the soup aisle, with cans on the floor, and I realized immediately what had happened. Mr. Forsyth's motto was "One-Stop Shopping," which meant he stuffed his shelves with as many different products as they could hold in hopes that people really would do all their shopping at his store. People didn't, but they did bump into the overloaded shelves, like I had a dozen times. Obviously that's what had happened to the young man.

I heard someone behind me and turned to see Bubba Jakes. Behind him, Mrs. Todd squinted through her thick glasses. I had smiled when I'd seen them before, but no one was smiling now.

"What are you doing, boy?" Mr. Forsyth demanded.

I happened to know that Mr. Forsyth was a softy deep down inside, but he sometimes put on a gruff front, especially if he thought it might impress one of his regular customers like Mrs. Todd.

"Sorry, sir," the young man mumbled. "I'll get it."

Janie pushed past us and crouched down beside him. "I can help," she said.

Mr. Forsyth grabbed her arm and pulled her up. "Let him do it."

"You shouldn't be here," Bubba told the young man. His voice was low and gruff, as if he was trying to act grown up, the way he'd been doing when he shopped for safety razors.

"Why not?" said Grant. "It's a free country."

Bubba grunted. The young man looked up at Grant, then gazed at me, as if he had a question but couldn't ask it. His face was open like a book, full of words and feelings if you knew how to read them. I tried to imagine what he was thinking but couldn't. It was like there was an invisible wall between us—white on one side, black on the other. It might seem strange to some people, but in Anniston we were used to it. That's just the way things were.

I wanted to tell him that. Grant was my friend, but

part of me agreed with Bubba. *Go home*, I thought. *This is our neighborhood, not yours.*

The young man turned back to the pyramid, carefully placing creamed celery on chicken gumbo, old-fashioned tomato on vegetable beef. When he finished, he got to his feet and nodded awkwardly.

"I'll be careful next time," he said.

"There won't be a next time," said Mr. Forsyth. "Leave, and don't come back."

The young man watched Mr. Forsyth. I saw something in his eyes—an impulse, a feeling—but I couldn't tell what it was. The two of them stared at each other for a long time, and finally the young man looked away. He turned, shoulders slumped, and left the store.

Mr. Forsyth shrugged, almost an apology.

"Personally, I don't mind them coming here," he said. "But they might bother some of my customers."

CHAPTER
THREE

She always kissed the baby first.

He was cute, I admit, but what about me? I was cute too, if you looked at me just right.

"Hi, Mama," I said.

"Hello, dear," she answered, barely looking up.

Mama had arrived home from the army depot, just down the hill and around the corner, where she worked as a secretary. She was wearing a suit with a neatly pressed blouse and scarf. To me, the suit looked stiff and scratchy. Mama didn't seem to mind though, about the suit or the work. If a job had to be done, she would do it. It was that simple.

Mama was like that. She didn't tell jokes and carry on like Daddy. He would be out in front, making noise and taking chances. She would come along behind, cleaning up, making things right, doing what needed to be done. With a strong jaw and clear blue eyes, she wasn't exactly pretty, but something about her was beautiful, especially when she set her mind on something. Her hair was the color of chocolate, and her smile, when she showed it, was surprising, like one of those warm spring days that come along sometimes in the winter.

She had started at the army depot after my father changed jobs with an insurance company in Anniston. I'd never been quite sure what had happened to my father's job. One day he was working at a desk in town, and the next he was out in the countryside, selling insurance to poor families, the way he'd done years ago when I was little.

I was embarrassed to ask Daddy about it, so I'd gone to Mama. That's how it was in my family. Daddy made things happen, and Mama explained, or tried to.

"Your father is good with people," she said. "You know that, don't you?"

I nodded. Daddy was always laughing and telling stories. If you wanted to find him, you just looked for where the people were.

"He did so well at sales, he was promoted to a desk job," Mama told me. "He sat in the office all day, shuffling papers and going to meetings. Hated it. Just hated it. One day he blew up in a meeting and yelled at his boss."

"Really? In the meeting?" It was hard to imagine Daddy blowing up at anybody, let alone his boss.

Mama nodded. "I think he planned it so he could get out of that office and back in the field. His boss was glad to oblige. People around town called it professional suicide. They shook their heads. Some of them laughed. Daddy didn't mind though. He was back on the road, meeting people, telling stories. Being Daddy."

"And you got a job."

"I like to keep busy," she said.

Now, arriving home, Mama set her purse on the rug and got down on her hands and knees, where the baby was squirming on a blanket. She pressed her lips against his bare stomach and blew, making a rude noise. I suppose it was adorable.

The baby's name was Royal. That's right, Royal. As in his highness. It happened to be my mother's maiden name, Mary Lou Royal, but that didn't make it right.

"He's a good little baby," said Lavender. "But, Lord, can he eat."

Lavender Jones stood by, watching. She was a large woman with coffee-colored skin and eyes that took in everything. Lavender had been our maid for fifteen years. She cleaned the house and cooked, and when I came along, she took care of me.

As far back as I could remember, Lavender had been there watching me, holding me, comforting me. She was Mama's extra pair of hands, extra smile. Daddy would go off on sales trips, leaving Mama, Lavender, and me. The three of us had our own little world. Then Daddy would come home, and the world shifted. I was happy to have him back, but Lavender wasn't. Daddy treated Lavender differently from the way Mama did. Mama asked; Daddy told. Mama helped; Daddy gave orders. Mama listened; Daddy looked away.

Lavender seemed distant when Daddy was around. She didn't smile or sing the way she did with me. She didn't hum to herself when she was cooking or tell stories when she was folding clothes. But Lavender always smiled when she saw Royal, even when Daddy was home. She loved that boy. She was like his second mother. Which was fine, except that I wanted her to be *my* second mother.

A few nights before, when Mama and Daddy thought I was asleep, I had heard them talking about Lavender.

"Can we afford to keep her?" Mama had asked.

"We're not poor," Daddy had replied.

"I think she's worried about her job," Mama had said finally.

"I'm working as hard as I can."

"I know, Charles. We both are."

I'd pictured Mama taking his hand and squeezing it the way you'd put pressure on a wound. He was quiet after that.

I lay in the darkness, staring up at the ceiling. They were talking about Lavender as if she was an employee. I knew better. She was family.

Mama kissed Royal's chubby cheek, then handed him to Lavender and headed for the bedroom to change. She came out a few minutes later wearing a sundress and sandals.

"Billie, did you finish your homework?" she asked.

"Yes, ma'am. Math and Latin, my two favorite subjects."

"Don't be a smart aleck, dear."

I heard a car pull up and hurried outside. Daddy drove a beat-up DeSoto that he'd bought from one of the neighbors. He was just climbing out, lugging his big briefcase. I wondered what he carried in there. Books? Bricks? A bowling ball?

I threw my arms around him, and he gave me a hug.

"How's my girl?" he asked.

"Tired of smelling diapers."

He chuckled. "Get used to it, sweetie."

I pulled back and looked at him. "You seem tired."

"I drove two hundred miles today. Insurance is a tough game."

Walking across the lawn, he shared his latest jokes with me. It was a little ritual we went through when he got home from work.

"What did one wall say to the other wall?" he asked me.

"I don't know."

"Let's meet in the corner. Why do cows wear bells?"

I shrugged. He grinned.

"Because their horns don't work."

Daddy got jokes by the dozen at Clyde's Hair Heaven, the barbershop where he went on Saturdays for his weekly trim. Most of the jokes weren't very good, but he said they helped to break the ice with customers. Besides, he enjoyed telling them. Daddy loved making people laugh.

"Make 'em laugh; then sign 'em up," he always said.

He spotted a football on the grass. Setting down his briefcase, he picked up the ball.

"Go long," he said.

I took off across the lawn, running as fast I could.

He lifted a spiral high into the air. I ran under it, and the ball dropped into my hands. I turned and lofted it back toward him. He snagged it, then flipped it back and forth from one hand to the other.

"I thought you were tired," I said.

"I'm insurance tired, not football tired."

Daddy had his quirks and faults. I guess we all do. But there was something that made most people like him. They gathered around, the way you would at a campfire on a chilly night. They sought him out, shared a joke, asked about the family, and left feeling better about themselves. Mama said it was a gift. Whatever it was, I was glad to be his daughter.

He set down the ball and picked up his briefcase. I came up beside him, and he put his hand on my shoulder. We walked across the lawn toward the house.

"So, Billie, are you helping your mama?"

"Sir?"

"She has a job now," he said. "She could use your help around the house."

"We have Lavender, don't we?"

"Lavender has plenty to do. Will you help out, Billie?"

"Yes, sir. I guess so."

As we crossed the porch, he stopped for a minute.

Glancing at the door, he whispered, "Oh, and have you thought about Mother's Day?"

"What do you mean?" I asked.

"It's a week from Sunday. You're a big girl now. You should do your own shopping. Buy something for your mama."

He opened his wallet and pulled out a five-dollar bill. "Next week sometime, go into town and pick out a present from you and Royal. While you're at it, get a card for me."

He pressed the bill into my hand, then planted an awkward kiss on my forehead. "There's my girl."

The minute we walked through the front door, Daddy made a beeline for the baby. He took Royal from Lavender and held him up like a prize pig.

"Will you look at this little guy?" asked Daddy.

Royal waved his arms and demonstrated what he did best—slobber. I swear, if you took him to the army depot, that kid could lubricate a tank.

Mama wiped the baby's mouth with a handkerchief.

"How was your day?" she asked.

Lavender smiled, and I saw a glimpse of the face she saved for Mama and me.

"His day was like most days," said Lavender. "Eat and poop."

Mama giggled. "I meant Mr. Sims."

"Me too," said Daddy. "Eat and poop. That pretty much says it all."

He gave the baby to Lavender, then set down his briefcase and eased into the La-Z-Boy recliner. Cranking the lever, he leaned back.

"Insurance is brutal," he said to no one in particular.

Mama came up behind him and rubbed his shoulders. I brought him the paper.

"Colavito hit a home run," I told him. "The Tigers won."

Besides Alabama football, Daddy and I followed the Birmingham Barons and their major league team, the Detroit Tigers. The Tigers had finished sixth the year before, but this season, led by their slugger Rocky Colavito, they were challenging the Yankees.

I knelt next to the La-Z-Boy, propped my elbow on the arm of the chair, and glanced through the paper with Daddy. The *Anniston Star* was published in the afternoons and on Sunday morning. Today it had stories about trouble in a place called Laos and about Alan Shepard, who was scheduled to be the first American in space if the weather in Florida would cooperate.

The first thing I always looked for, though, was the local articles. Sure enough, there was one about Anniston teachers holding a meeting downtown. I wasn't interested in the article as much as the name at the top: Tom McCall, Grant's dad, the reporter who covered most of the local stories. Seeing his name there made me feel good, like I knew someone important.

Lavender gave the baby a hug, set him on her hip, and headed for the kitchen.

Daddy asked her, "What's for supper?"

"Fried chicken," she said.

"Again?"

I said, "It's good. I love it."

"How about a steak?" he called after her. "You know what that is?"

He grinned at me and winked. I looked away. I didn't like it when he teased Lavender.

She called over her shoulder, "You give me a steak, I'll cook it."

Before she turned away, an expression flickered across her face. Whatever it was, I realized it was the same thing I'd seen in the eyes of the young man at the grocery—something dark and mysterious, like anger pushed down and covered up.

Daddy must have seen it too. He lowered the paper. "Lavender, is there something you want to say?"

She shook her head. "Don't mind me, Mr. Sims. I'm just talking."

Daddy studied her for a minute, then looked over at Mama.

"You know what?" he said. "Steak sounds good."

Taking his wallet from his back pocket, he counted out a few dollars and waved them at Lavender.

"Here's some money," he told her. "Go down to Forsyth's and buy the best steak in the place."

Mama said, "Charles, really—"

"Then bring it back here and cook it. How does that sound?"

Sometimes Daddy's teasing turned into something else, something hard and mean. It made me mad, but I didn't know what to do about it.

Mama came up behind Daddy and touched his shoulder. "She made some fried chicken. Let's have that."

Lavender reached out with her free hand and took the money.

"Yes, sir, Mr. Sims," she said. "Whatever you say."

Royal, who for once had been forgotten, started to cry. Mama took him off Lavender's hip and gave him a kiss. Daddy watched as Lavender whipped off her apron, picked up her purse, and headed for the door.

Daddy looked at Mama. Mama looked back. Royal screamed.

I said, "I'm going with Lavender."

CHAPTER
FOUR

It would have been a long walk down the hill and an even longer walk back, so we took Lavender's car, a green Studebaker that wasn't much older than our DeSoto. The difference was that Daddy parked in the driveway, and Lavender parked on the street in front. I saw her pull into the driveway once, but Daddy, like a traffic cop, had motioned her back.

Lavender crossed the lawn, got into her car, and pulled the door shut. I climbed in the other side. Lavender gripped the steering wheel, closed her eyes, and sighed.

"That man," she said.

"You don't like steak?" I asked.

"It's not about steak. It's about who's boss."

"It is?"

"Who gives the orders and who takes them. He can't be the boss at work, so he wants to be at home. He's showing me who's in charge."

"You make it sound like a job," I said.

"Oh, it's a job. It surely is."

Hearing her say that made me sad. "What about family?"

"I love your family, Billie. But it's yours, not mine."

I tried to picture Lavender's family. The frame was empty, like Grant's frames before he put photos in them.

"I really do like your fried chicken," I said.

Lavender pulled her keys from her purse, then glanced over at me. "You're a nice girl, Billie. You always have been."

She started the car and headed down the hill. The car smelled like Lavender—a special combination of soap, starch, and something else I couldn't identify. We were in her world now, and she seemed more relaxed.

"Mama's nice," I said. "So is Daddy. We're all nice."

Lavender nodded wearily. "That's what they say."

She reached into her purse and popped a cherry Life Saver into her mouth. Maybe that was the other smell I'd noticed. She sucked on the Life Saver while she drove, as if she was considering something.

"You know what prejudice is?" she asked.

"Prejudice? Is it liking one thing over another?"

"Not just things—people. Rich over poor. White over black. Happens all the time. Some of the nicest people do it."

I had to think about that one. "Then those people aren't nice, are they?"

Lavender looked at me, then back at the road. "My friend Corea, she has a theory about prejudice. She says it's a disease like mumps or whooping cough. You catch it from your parents and friends. Most people never recover."

"Do I have it?" I asked.

A shadow flickered across her face. "Yes, sweetheart, I'm afraid you do. The question is, will you pass it on?"

How do you pass on prejudice? Do you eat from the same dishes, drink from the same glass? I thought of the separate drinking fountains around town for white and colored. We were afraid of catching something, that was for sure. Maybe that fear was prejudice. Maybe the disease was being afraid.

As we pulled into the parking lot at Forsyth's, a Greyhound bus swept down the hill past us, kicking up dust.

I checked my watch. "That's the five thirty-two,"

I said. "Last bus of the day—to Birmingham, then Tupelo."

Lavender snorted. "I swear, your head is full of schedules."

She eyed me thoughtfully, then seemed to make a decision. If the young man in the grocery was an open book, she was a closed one. There was a story inside, but it was hard to read. Then, every once in a while, something would pop out and surprise you.

She said, "You like buses so much? I got some bus news for you."

"Bus news?"

"Negroes sit in the back, right?"

I shrugged. "That's the way it's always been."

"Well, it's about to change. There's a group that won't sit in the back. They're called Freedom Riders, and they're coming on Greyhound. They'll sit with the white folks—in the waiting room, on the bus, at the lunch counter."

"Isn't that against the law?"

"In Alabama, yes. But these folks are coming from Washington, DC, black and white together. They'll cross state lines. You know what that means?"

"Not really."

"Once they cross state lines, the U.S. government makes the laws." There was something about the way

she said the words that made them glitter in the air—
U.S. government, like when my Sunday school teacher
said *Jesus*. "And the U.S. government says no one has to
sit in back."

I thought of my dad and his friends down at Clyde's
Hair Heaven. "That wouldn't go over too well around
here."

"We'll find out, won't we?" said Lavender.

"What do you mean?"

"The Freedom Riders are coming to Anniston," she
said. "They'll be at the Greyhound station next Sunday,
on Mother's Day."

* * *

Besides being a grocery store, Forsyth's was home to
the Tall Tales Club. It was a group of older men who got
together late in the day, drank coffee, and told stories.
Most of the stories weren't true, of course, and that was
the point. Along the way, they also talked about what
was going on in Anniston and whatever else was on
their minds.

That afternoon, I walked into the store and saw
them sitting in their usual spot, a rickety table by the
produce section. The club president was Uncle Harvey
Caldwell, who wasn't my uncle or anybody else's as far
as I knew, but that's what we called him.

"Hey, Billie," said Uncle Harvey when he saw me. "We were just talking about the Crimson Tide. Any predictions?"

I grinned. "They'll win it all."

That started a hubbub among the other club members. There were five of them that day—five and a half if you counted Jokester, a six-year-old neighborhood boy who liked to hide under the table—and Alabama football was one subject they all had opinions on.

The hubbub stopped when Lavender followed me in. She didn't come to Forsyth's very often, since Mama usually did our grocery shopping on the way home from work. The Tall Tales Club watched as Lavender approached the meat counter, where Mr. Forsyth was putting out some hamburger. He eyed her nervously, aware that some of his best customers were watching.

"I need the best steak you got, please, sir," Lavender told him.

"Is that so?"

She pulled the money from her purse and set it on the counter. "It's for Mr. Sims."

Mr. Forsyth glanced at Uncle Harvey, then back at Lavender. "So why did he send you?"

The men around the table chuckled. They seemed to be laughing at Lavender, and I didn't understand why.

Lavender closed her eyes for a moment, then opened them again.

"One steak, please," she said.

Mr. Forsyth watched her, then said, "Coming right up." He bent over the counter and sorted through the steaks.

As he did, Uncle Harvey wandered over and leaned up against the meat counter. He spoke to Mr. Forsyth but gazed at Lavender. "So, Richard, I hear you had a little altercation at the store today."

"Wasn't nothing," Mr. Forsyth said.

"Nothing? A Negro boy sasses you and destroys some goods?"

I waited for Lavender to answer, but she just stared straight ahead.

I wanted to say, "That's not true! It was an accident." Somehow, though, I couldn't form the words.

Uncle Harvey asked Lavender, "What do you think? Were you there?"

"No, sir," she said, still staring.

"Just as well," he said. "You got your place; we got ours. Right?"

Lavender blinked a couple of times real fast but didn't say anything.

"Right?" said Uncle Harvey.

The store was dead quiet. I heard Uncle Harvey's rough breathing. He had asthma, and everybody in town knew it.

"Except for the Freedom Riders," I said.

Uncle Harvey swung his gaze in my direction. The others looked at me too.

"Freedom Riders?" he said.

Lavender shot me a look. Suddenly I was unsure of myself, but I managed to keep going.

"They're coming to Anniston next Sunday," I stammered. "They'll be at the Greyhound station. They'll sit in the front of the bus, black and white together. It's interstate commerce. That's a different kind of law."

Uncle Harvey stared at me. So did the other men. Lavender gazed at the floor, shaking her head.

"Here's your steak," Mr. Forsyth said to Lavender. His face looked whiter than when we 'd walked in. Hers looked darker.

She paid him, then headed for the door. "Come on, child," she told me.

Uncle Harvey and his friends watched as we left the store. Nobody said a word.

In the car, I turned to Lavender. "I messed up, didn't I?"

Lavender sighed. "They would have found out. Anyway, it shouldn't be a secret. The Freedom Riders would thank you. They want everyone to know. They even put it in the newspaper."

That made me feel better, but I was still uneasy. By telling Uncle Harvey and the others, I'd given them information, and in the wrong hands, information could be a weapon.

When we got home, Lavender cooked up the steak for Daddy and put it on a plate. He sat down to dinner and enjoyed every bite of it. Mama and I had fried chicken.

Lavender wasn't feeling well, so I told her I would wash the dishes, and she left. I stood at the sink, thinking about my town. It was home, and I loved it. I could sit down and talk all day long with people like Uncle Harvey Caldwell and the Tall Tales Club. We would laugh and tell stories and poke fun at each other. We shared a history and a way of looking at things. But today, in Lavender's eyes, I had seen a different place. It could be thoughtless and mean. It could be dangerous.

In just a few days, a group of people would get on a bus and come riding through Anniston. Lavender said they were clearing a path, sweeping the road clean. But there were people in town who felt differently, and I had helped them.

I tried to imagine the Freedom Riders—brave,

strong, sure of their dream. Maybe they would change my town. Maybe they would change my family. Maybe they would change me.

CHAPTER
FIVE

Lavender called the next morning, saying she felt sick and wouldn't be coming to our house. I remembered the look on her face in Forsyth's, when Uncle Harvey was talking to her. Maybe that's when she had started to feel bad.

Thinking back on it, I realized this had happened before. When there were disagreements or cross words, Lavender wouldn't say anything. She would set her mouth in a firm line and her eyes would go dead, and the next day she would stay home. It was like she was holding her thoughts inside, and the thoughts made her sick. I wondered what kind of thoughts would do that to you.

Mama hung up the phone and headed back to the

breakfast table, shaking her head. "What about the baby? I can't take him to work."

I was putting jam on my toast, and Daddy, in a tie and shirtsleeves, was finishing the last of his coffee. Royal sat in a high chair, where Mama had been feeding him. He let out a cry, and Daddy smiled.

"Smart kid. He knows. No Lavender today."

"I wonder if Grace would help," said Mama. Grace was Mrs. McCall, who was home during the day.

Mama checked and learned that Mrs. McCall could watch Royal, but only until three o'clock, when she'd be taking Grant to the dentist. Mama said that luckily it was a light day at work and she could leave early. As she told us, Daddy shot me a meaningful look. I didn't understand for a minute; then I remembered our conversation in the front yard.

"Oh yeah. I guess I could help," I said. "I'll be home from school."

"That would be nice, dear," said Mama.

And that's how, later that day, I ended up wiping Royal's face and other body parts. When Mama got home, we had gone to the McCalls' and picked up the baby. We had played with him for a few minutes and then, when Grant and his mom had left for the dentist, we took Royal home.

Somehow I got the job of feeding him. Basically, the idea was to try and get more into his mouth than came out. I sat in front of his high chair, spooning mushed-up peaches from a little jar, and he did everything he could think of but eat. He cooed and clapped and grabbed my nose. When he got it, he squeezed.

"Ow!" I said.

Mama, whose workday hadn't been as light as she'd hoped, had brought home some papers and was shuffling them at the breakfast table. She smiled at Royal. "You little goober."

I might have picked a different word, but I didn't say it. I'd been thinking about something else. "Mama, are we prejudiced?"

She looked at me. "What kind of question is that? Of course not."

"I heard it's like the mumps. You catch it and pass it on."

"It's a choice," she said. "In our family we choose to treat people with kindness and respect."

"People like Lavender?"

"That's right," said Mama.

"She's part of the family, isn't she?"

"Of course."

That made me feel better. I wondered how Lavender

was feeling. I pictured her bundled up in front of her TV watching soap operas, which she called "the stories." We used to watch them together when I was little. She said the stories helped her escape to another place. I was hoping to do the same thing someday, only I would use a bus.

"When Lavender gets on the bus," I said, "why does she have to sit in back?"

"You're full of questions, aren't you?"

"I was just wondering."

Mama studied me, then asked, "What do you think?"

"It's the law," I said. "Also, it's tradition."

"That's right," she said. "And there's something else. I think people are more comfortable when they're separated. They like being with their own kind."

I'd heard that before. I'd said it myself a few times. But now, thinking about the Freedom Riders, I wondered if it was true. We said all kinds of things about Negroes—what they liked, what they thought, what they believed. If we really wanted to know, why didn't we ask them?

Royal squirmed in his high chair, and I realized the little jar of baby food was empty. The question was, were there more peaches inside his body or on the outside? I dampened a washcloth and used it to clean him up, while he lunged for my nose.

"I'm not very good at this," I said.

"You're fine, dear," said Mama. "And while you're at it, could you please change his diaper?"

I sighed and took Royal into his room, where I wrestled him on the changing table. I think he won. Afterward, he looked up at me, burped, and fell asleep. I laid him gently in his crib and returned to the kitchen.

"Did you lose something?" asked Mama, seeing that I wasn't holding Royal.

"He's taking a nap. I wish I could fall asleep that fast."

I went to the fridge and got two bottles of RC Cola. I opened them and put one in front of Mama, then took a gulp from the other one and plopped down at the table.

"Thank you, sweetheart," said Mama. Gathering up her papers, she put them in her briefcase and took a sip of the RC.

"The McCalls don't have a maid," I said.

"Mrs. McCall doesn't work."

"Grant told me they don't believe in maids."

Mama chuckled. "That's like saying they don't believe in cornbread or black-eyed peas."

"He says maids work too hard and don't get paid enough."

"Sweetheart, the McCalls are new to town. They'll learn."

"I'm not so sure. You know how Mr. McCall is."

"He's a fine person. So is Grant. Speaking of Grant, how's he doing these days?"

"Grant? He can't see what's right in front of him, unless it's in his viewfinder."

"I think he likes you."

"What?" I said. "Oh, please."

I remembered the way Grant had shown me how to use the camera, with his cheek next to mine and lemonade on his breath.

Mama said, "You're changing, Billie. You're a lovely young lady."

I took another swig of RC. I didn't feel lovely. I felt hot and awkward and confused. I liked Grant but he drove me nuts. I loved my town but wanted to get out. I wanted to grow up but didn't know how.

CHAPTER SIX

We lived on the Birmingham Highway, but the funny thing was, we almost never went to Birmingham. Mama said it was too big, and besides, we had everything we needed right there in Anniston. And Daddy? He was tired. He was always tired.

All of that changed on Saturday. If you lived in our neighborhood, Birmingham was the place to be, because that was the location of the state spelling bee. It was held in the gym at the YWCA, a big, old brick building downtown that had an arched doorway with pillars above it.

The gym was on the second floor, and when we walked inside, we were hit by a wave of sound—kids chattering, families visiting, chairs scraping on the wooden floor. It was a big, high-ceilinged room with dark wood halfway up the walls. Someone had set up a stage at the front, with chairs for the spellers and a microphone.

The spellers were milling around in front of the stage, and I spotted Janie Forsyth off to one side, shifting nervously from foot to foot. She was a shy girl, but then it occurred to me that all the spellers must be shy—a whole group of kids who were more comfortable with words than with people.

Nearby, Mr. McCall was on the job. He was short and pudgy, but that didn't mean he was weak. According to Grant, some local crooks and a few politicians had found that out the hard way. Mr. McCall wandered among the spellers, asking questions and writing the answers in a little notebook. Grant followed along behind, taking pictures.

Today one of those spellers would become state champion, winning a set of the *Encyclopedia Britannica*, a $250 radio, and an engraved writing pen. Best of all, the winner would get a trip to the national spelling bee, to be held the following month in Washington, DC. I tried to imagine going there, or maybe traveling to New York to visit Miss Harper Lee. Cities stretched in front of me, the way they'd been spread out below Alan Shepard the day before, when he became the first American in space. The world was bigger than Anniston or even Birmingham. Now we knew it was bigger than Earth too.

There was a long table at the back of the room where people served cookies and punch. The rest of the place was filled with folding chairs lined up in rows. I saw Mrs. McCall sitting near the stage with the Forsyth family, and we headed in their direction. I took a seat next to Mrs. McCall, who greeted me with a hug. Daddy filed in behind me, and Mama, with the baby, took a place next to him.

As we settled in, I was surprised to see a group of Negro students sitting near the back of the room. Mama noticed where I was looking and leaned over toward me.

"They're from Cobb Avenue High," she said. "I heard about them at work. They came to watch, hoping to be part of the bee someday. You know, because of the court decision."

The court decision was *Brown versus the Board of Education*. The teachers at school hadn't mentioned the decision, but Mr. McCall had explained it to me. In 1954, the U.S. Supreme Court had ruled that segregated schools were illegal—that having separate schools wasn't allowed, even if they were equal. The schools would have to integrate.

"Then how come we're still segregated?" I had asked him.

Mr. McCall had gazed at me, a thoughtful expression on his face. "I've been asking the school board that same question. They haven't given me a good answer."

"Do you really think black and white kids could go to school together?"

"They'll have to," he had said, "eventually."

"That would be fine with me," I had told him. "I just wonder about other people. Some of them might not like it."

As I remembered the words, Mr. Forsyth's comment echoed in my head. *I don't mind them coming here, but they might bother some of my customers.*

If integration was okay with Mr. Forsyth and okay with me, who were all those other people?

I thought back to that day in the store and realized something. In spite of what he had said, Mr. Forsyth didn't feel comfortable with Negroes in his store. He just didn't want to admit it, so he blamed his customers.

Maybe I was doing the same thing. I wondered what it would be like to have Negroes at my school. The thought made me uneasy, but I wasn't sure why. It was just a feeling I had, and thoughts bubbled up after it. They had their schools, and we had ours. Why did we have to mix? I was ashamed to admit it, but somewhere deep down inside, it was how I felt. I had blamed other people for segregation, but maybe I was one of them.

I glanced uneasily at the group of Negro students and saw a familiar face. It was the young man from the store. Like the others, he was nicely dressed, wearing a coat and tie. I thought of him at Forsyth's, and I imagined him at my school. Somehow it bothered me.

Next to the young man, wearing the kind of dress you might wear to church, a girl was staring at me. She was my age, with skin the color of copper and a pale blue ribbon in her hair. At first I thought her gaze was simple curiosity, but when she kept staring, I realized it was more than that. The gaze was proud and defiant, and it was directed at me. She watched me all the way to my seat and kept watching. Finally, when I went to the drinking fountain, I looked up and saw her standing nearby.

"Do I know you?" I asked.

She said, "You're Billie Sims. You're a tomboy, and your next-door neighbor is Grant McCall."

Now it was my turn to stare. "Who told you that?"

"You go to Wellborn High. You ride your bike to school, you read the newspaper, and your room is a mess."

"Who are you?" I asked.

Her eyes were brown, almost black. Suddenly I realized I'd seen them before but in a different face, one as familiar as my own.

"Lavender," I said.

The girl gave a little nod. "I'm Jarmaine Jones, Lavender's daughter."

I guess I had known that Lavender had a daughter, but it was a shock to see her standing there.

"You know all about me," I said, "but I don't know anything about you."

Jarmaine studied me, waiting. I thought she might tell me something, but she didn't.

Finally she said, "I heard what happened at the grocery store." She glanced toward her group of friends, where the young man was watching us.

"That's Bradley," she said. "He's one of the best students at Cobb High. Now he can't go into that store."

"I saw it," I said. "It was an accident. He didn't mean anything."

"Did you say that?"

"At the store? Well, no."

"Why not?" she asked.

Because they were adults. Because I would get in trouble. Because in my town you just didn't do that.

I shrugged. "It's not my store."

Spinning on her heel, Jarmaine turned and walked away.

Why was she upset? I was trying to be nice. Couldn't she tell?

About that time, one of the judges tapped on the microphone, and I hurried to my seat. The contest was starting. The spellers took their places on the stage, where Grant snapped their pictures. Then the contestants were called up, one by one, and given words.

Janie sailed through the first couple of rounds, but I couldn't imagine how. I'd never heard such words: Precipitous? Jejune? Cloture? Where did they come from? Obviously Janie's dictionary was different from mine.

As spellers missed words, the group got smaller. Finally, after two hours and over twenty rounds, the only people left were Janie and a girl from Montgomery named Charlotte Campbell. Then Charlotte missed, and it was up to Janie.

Mama grabbed my hand and held on for dear life. Down the row, Mrs. McCall was sweating, and it looked like Mr. Forsyth was about to have a heart attack.

The judge read Janie's word: "Cloisonne."

I glanced at Daddy. He looked at me and raised his palms. We were clueless.

Amazingly, Janie wasn't. With confidence she said,

"Cloisonne: *C-L-O-I-S-O-N-N-E*."

The judge boomed, "We've got our winner!"

Janie grinned. We leaped to our feet, cheering. The judge raised her hand high, like she was heavyweight champion of the world.

He leaned down to the microphone and said to Janie, "If you give me your address, we'll mail your prizes. Congratulations!"

Janie thanked him, waved to the crowd, and started to walk off. But the contest wasn't over. As we turned to leave, someone tapped the microphone, and a young girl's voice boomed out over the loudspeaker.

"Hello. Excuse me."

I looked back and saw Jarmaine standing onstage.

"My name is Jarmaine Jones," she said. "I'd like to say something."

All around me, people stopped and stared, including Mama and Daddy. At first I wondered if they knew who she was, but from their expressions, it was clear they didn't.

Jarmaine seemed nervous but determined. She took a deep breath, then said, "We have a white champion. Now let's find out the state champion."

The crowd erupted. Down the row, Mama and Daddy frowned.

Jarmaine didn't budge. She nodded, and the young man I'd seen at the store strode up onstage.

She said, "This is Bradley Thomas, the spelling champion of Cobb High. We challenge you to a runoff."

"Get 'em out of there!" someone shouted.

The judge, who had walked away, stepped back onstage and leaned in to the microphone. "Sorry about this, folks. We'll take care of it. The contest is over."

Jarmaine said, "It's not over. It's only half a contest."

"Young lady—" said the judge.

Bradley Thomas came up behind them. "Sir, what's wrong? If your winner is such a good speller, what are you afraid of?"

The judge said, "If you want to be in the contest, send me a letter."

"So you can disregard it," Bradley said. "Disregard: *D-I-S-R-E-G-A-R-D*."

"We're not going to spell," said the judge. "The spelling is over."

Bradley said, "You can't prevent it. Prevent: *P-R-E-V-E-N-T*."

"Stop that!" said the judge.

Jarmaine grabbed the microphone back. "Ignorance: *I-G-N-O-R-A-N-C-E*. Prejudice: *P-R-E-J-U-D-I-C-E*. Segregation: *S-E-G-R-E-G-A-T-I-O-N*."

With each word, there were more shouts. Some of the men in the audience edged toward the stage. As they got closer, Bradley chimed in. "Liberty: *L-I-B-E-R-T-Y*. America: *A-M-E-R-I-C-A*."

The other Negro students, who had been drifting toward the stage, mounted the steps and surrounded their friends. There were more angry shouts from the audience. The judge looked around desperately.

Out of the crowd, a small figure appeared. He tucked a notepad into his pocket and climbed the steps. It was Mr. McCall. Jarmaine said something to the other students. They stepped aside, and he approached the microphone.

"Folks," he said, "it's been a good contest, and we've got our state champion."

The Negro students murmured unhappily.

"But these kids have a point," he went on. "I propose that next year, we expand the contest and let everyone participate."

Bradley called out, "Participate: *P-A-R-T-I-C-I-P-A-T-E*."

Jarmaine grinned and shouted, "Victory: *V-I-C-T-O-R-Y*."

The Negro students cheered.

The judge stepped back up to the microphone. "We'll consider it," he said.

CHAPTER SEVEN

The crowd spilled out of the YWCA, still buzzing. Daddy glanced over at Mama and shook his head.

"What a shame. It was Janie's day, and they stole the spotlight from her."

He didn't have to say who "they" were.

"Why weren't they in the spelling bee to start with?" I asked.

"They've never been in it," said Mama.

I thought about what Mr. McCall had said. "What do you think it'll be like next year?"

"Maybe there won't be a next year," said Daddy.

Mama rolled her eyes. "Charles, it's just spelling. Anyway, it's not like they were carrying guns."

There was a flash, and I looked up. Grant was

hurrying around with his camera, taking pictures of us and the other people in the crowd. He snapped a few last photos, then joined us as we headed for the car.

"What did you think of Jarmaine Jones?" Grant asked.

"You know her?" said Daddy.

"She's Lavender's daughter," I said.

Daddy's eyes opened wide.

"Oh my goodness," said Mama.

Grant said, "I met her at the *Star*. She's a student intern there. They've had an internship program with Cobb High for a couple of years now. Jarmaine just started. Sometimes she helps my dad with his stories. He tells me she's good."

Mama said, "She has nerve, I'll give her that."

Daddy shook his head. I couldn't tell if he was amazed or disgusted. Maybe both.

I dropped back beside Grant and lowered my voice. "I met her before the spelling bee. She seemed angry."

He said, "Think about how Negroes must feel. Their fathers and brothers fought in the war, and when they came home, nothing had changed. Separate but equal. Colored only. The courts say it's illegal, but we keep right on doing it. Then all the little things, like the spelling contest. Wouldn't it make you mad?"

I didn't know how to answer. It was like trying to play a game when you didn't understand the rules.

* * *

Larry Crabtree understood the rules and thought it was his duty to enforce them. That's what he was doing at school on Monday when I went looking for Grant. I found the two of them tangled up on the floor in front of Grant's locker, with a group of students gathered around, watching.

Larry yelled, "Got it?"

Grant said, "No!"

Larry slugged him.

"Got it?"

"No!"

Larry slugged him again.

I jumped on Larry's back and started pounding him on the shoulders.

"Hey!" he screeched.

I put a choke hold on his neck, and when he reached back to stop me, Grant gave him a shove and struggled to stand up. I let go and stood next to Grant, facing Larry.

"What's going on?" I asked Grant.

"They're mad at my father. They don't like what he did on Saturday."

Larry said, "We don't want any Negroes in our spelling bee."

"You weren't even there!" I told him. "There was going to be trouble. Mr. McCall stopped it. You should be thanking Grant, not beating him up."

"They're trying to change things," said Larry. "We like the way things are—white on one side, black on the other."

Grant said, "White on top, black on the bottom."

"Maybe," grunted Larry. He gathered up his books and motioned to his friends. They moved off down the hall like they owned it. It made me want to hit him again.

I turned to Grant. "Are you okay?"

"Yeah." He rubbed his cheek, where a bruise was starting to develop.

I said, "Larry Crabtree's an idiot."

"He's scared," said Grant. "They all are."

I reached out to touch the bruise. Grant flinched.

"Hold still," I said.

I ran my fingers over the bruise, then pulled a tissue from my pocket, moistened it on my tongue, and wiped the dirt from his cheek, the way I'd seen Mama do. It felt good, like I was taking care of him.

His chin was strong and his eyes were bright. Sometimes they were angry, like when he thought people weren't being fair. Today, up close, I saw something new and giggled.

"What are all these little hairs?"

He pulled away. "Stop it."

I leaned in and ran my fingers across his chin. It felt rough.

"They're whiskers!" I crowed.

He looked around, embarrassed. "Hey, shut up."

"Grant McCall has puberty!" I said.

Actually, I thought it was pretty cool. I didn't know how to tell him though, so I kept quiet. He headed off down the hall, shaking his head. I hurried after him and stuck close for the rest of the day, watching for Larry Crabtree and his friends. Maybe Grant didn't like me touching his cheek, but he didn't mind having me in a fight.

After school I found Grant sitting by his locker, studying the baseball card he had bought on Friday. It showed a picture of Frank Robinson on the front and his statistics on the back.

"Guess what Robinson hit last year," said Grant. "Two ninety-seven. How many home runs? Thirty-one. How many triples?"

"Hey," I said, "give me a chance to answer."

"Okay, how many triples?"

"I don't care," I said.

He glared at me. It was part of our ongoing baseball war. I was a Detroit Tigers fan, and Grant rooted for the Cincinnati Reds, from the city where he had grown up.

Shaking his head, Grant got the camera from his locker, slung it over his shoulder, and walked with me to the bike rack. I liked it when we rode home together, telling what had happened during the day and complaining about assignments. I didn't like it when he went off by himself, riding his bike or taking pictures or spending time with anyone but me.

I asked him, "Want to go downtown?"

"Why?" he said.

"I have an errand to run. Plus, I want to see your dad."

"You're not going to tell him about Larry Crabtree, are you?"

When Grant had problems, he didn't go running to his parents. I'd always admired him for that.

I shook my head. "No, it's something else."

Grant shrugged. "Let's go."

He loaded his books onto the metal carrier behind his bicycle seat. I did the same. Then we swung up onto our bikes and headed out of the parking lot, past the football field and the sign that said *Home of the Panthers*.

Wellborn High, made up of brick buildings on a hillside several miles west of town, was still pretty new. It had been built a few years earlier when the army depot had expanded, bringing hundreds of new families into the area. It seemed funny that we had decided to call ourselves the Panthers, because everyone knew that Cobb High, the Negro school, was known as the Mighty Panthers and had been for years.

Grant and I pedaled down Eulaton Road, past pin oaks and loblolly pines, until it flattened out and turned into Tenth Street. As it did, we got a good view of Anniston, where the tallest buildings were churches. Anniston was beautiful and it was my home, but I still found myself looking over the steeples and wondering what lay beyond.

We found Mr. McCall at his desk, hunched over a typewriter with boxes stacked on the floor all around him. It had been almost a year since the *Anniston Star* moved to its new headquarters, but he'd been too busy writing to unpack.

The new building, on Tenth Street at the edge of town, was made of bricks and glass, with a white rectangle jutting out over the entrance. It was just one story tall but covered most of a city block, with the reporters and sales offices up front and a big open area in back for the presses. Mr. McCall had walked Grant and me back there once to see the presses pounding away like pile drivers, churning out the news.

Mr. McCall looked up from his typewriter and smiled.

"Hey, kids. What brings you here?"

"I liked your article about Janie," I told him.

For years, the only time I had read the newspaper was when Daddy and I checked the sports section. But when Grant and his family moved next door, I had started reading the articles by Mr. McCall. This one had appeared on the front page of the Sunday edition, the day after the spelling bee. It had described the contest, as well as what had happened afterward. In Mr. McCall's articles, even if you knew the subject, you always learned something. In the case of Janie, I found out she was excited about facing the Negro students next year.

I nodded toward Mr. McCall's typewriter. "What are you working on now?"

His face lit up. "It's about the first American in space, Alan Shepard. You know, the local angle. After all, Huntsville is just a couple of hours up the road."

Thanks to Mr. McCall's stories, I knew about

Huntsville. They called it the Rocket City. A rocket designed there had launched America's first satellite, Explorer 1. Just the year before, they had opened a big space center there, run by a scientist named Wernher von Braun.

"Where do you get all that information?" I asked.

He chuckled. "That's the best part of the job. I ask questions."

"Miss Hobbs, our English teacher, says to write about what you know."

"For me, it's just the opposite," he said. "I write about what I don't know and want to find out. So I learn something every day."

I thought about all the things I didn't know. Why do I hate homework? How do you throw a curve? What's it like to live in New York City? Why do people get mad when you try to be nice?

"Hey," I said, trying to sound casual, "I heard that Jarmaine Jones works here."

"That's right. Sometimes she helps me out. Jarmaine's good." He glanced around. "She was here a minute ago."

I lowered my voice. "Can I ask you something? How come Cobb High has an internship program and Wellborn doesn't? I wouldn't mind working here myself. And I know Grant wants to. Right, Grant?"

I glanced over and saw that he was fooling with his camera. I poked him with my elbow. "Right, Grant?"

"Huh? Yeah, I guess."

Mr. McCall shrugged. "That's no big secret. Mr. Ayers, the owner of the *Star*, believes in equal rights for Negroes. He thought the program would help the students at Cobb, and the paper too."

"Some people call it the *Red Star*," I said. "You know, like communist."

I thought Mr. McCall might laugh. Instead, he leaned toward me, his expression full of feeling.

"Don't you believe it, Billie. Equal rights isn't communist. It's as American as you or me. Or Jarmaine."

I glanced around, partly to avoid his glare but mostly to look for Jarmaine. She wasn't there.

Just then, David Franklin walked by. He was a staff photographer and one of Grant's heroes.

"Hey, Mr. Franklin," said Grant. "I got that new lens, like you suggested."

The next thing I knew, he and Grant were lost in conversation. Figuring Grant would be busy for a while, I turned to Mr. McCall. "There's something I need to do. I'll be back in a few minutes."

He straightened his shoulders. "Sorry about my little outburst. That stuff about the *Red Star* gets my goat."

"It's okay. I'm glad you care so much about your job. I hope I care that much someday."

Mr. McCall smiled, then turned back to his typewriter, ready to learn.

CHAPTER EIGHT

I went through the lobby and out the door. Next to the entrance was a bench, and on it sat Jarmaine.

She wore a simple peach-colored dress and was eating a snack from a brown paper bag. I recognized the snack. It was peanut-butter crackers, the kind Lavender made for me. I imagined Lavender getting up early to fix Jarmaine's lunch before she came to our house. I wondered what it would be like to run two households and juggle two lives.

I hesitated by the bench. "I just wanted to talk."

Jarmaine eyed me warily. "About what?"

"You seemed mad when we talked at the spelling bee. You know, about the grocery."

Jarmaine's eyes flashed. "You were there. You could

have said something."

"Like what?"

"This is wrong. It isn't fair."

"Mr. Forsyth owns the grocery," I said. "He wanted your friend to leave."

"It's a store! You can't pick and choose your customers. You just open the doors and let people in."

"He's actually a very nice man," I said.

There was that word again: *nice*. Was Mr. Forsyth nice? Was I?

"He's a cracker," said Jarmaine.

I'd heard the term at school, whispered in the hallways. A cracker was ignorant, like a redneck or poor white trash. I'd never heard a Negro say it before.

Jarmaine sighed and shook her head. "Mama doesn't like me calling people names. She says if we do it, they'll call us names too."

I studied Jarmaine. She had her mother's eyes, but there was a difference. When Lavender was angry or scared, her face was like a mask. You couldn't tell what she was thinking. But something about Jarmaine's face let you see right through. It made me nervous, and when I'm nervous, I talk. I needed something to say and remembered what Grant had told me after the spelling bee.

"Look, I know you're upset," I said. "After all, your

father was in the war; then he came home and nothing had changed. Separate but equal. Colored only."

"My father left when I was a baby," Jarmaine said. "I never met him."

I looked around for something to crawl under. Maybe the bench. Maybe I could just lift up the lawn and pull it over me.

I said, "Am I blushing? I do that sometimes. Do Negroes blush? How can you tell?"

I wanted to shut up but couldn't. "Do you get sunburned? If you can't see it, is it really a burn? What about zits? Can you stop me, please? Can you just grab my foot and pull it out of my mouth?"

She stared at me for the longest time. Then she laughed. Not giggles or chuckles, but big laughs. Finally, after a long time, she stopped.

"Yes. Yes. And yes," she said.

"Pardon me?"

"We blush. We sunburn. And, I can personally tell you, we have zits."

"I'm a jerk," I said.

"My mother told me you have a good heart," said Jarmaine. She offered me a cracker. I ate it in one big gulp, the way I always did.

"Those are my favorites," I said. "She makes them

for me too."

"I don't like sharing her," said Jarmaine.

I don't know why that surprised me. In a way it made sense. I didn't like sharing my things or my friends. But sharing Lavender was different, like sharing the sun.

I said, "So, you're an intern."

She nodded. "They pick two of us at school each year. I was lucky."

"Mr. McCall says you're good."

"He's a good reporter," she said. "I like helping him."

"He lives next door to me."

"I know," said Jarmaine. "I know all about you."

That made me feel funny, like there was some kind of shadow world next to mine, where Jarmaine lived and watched.

"There are some things you don't know," I said.

"Like what?"

"All kinds of things. My dreams."

Jarmaine gazed off into the distance. "Let's see. You dream of a house. A husband. Kids playing in the yard."

I smiled. "Nope. I dream about going to Montgomery or maybe New York or Washington, DC. I'd meet new people, try new things. I'd do whatever I wanted to."

"Such as?"

"Things. Big things. Be a writer."

The idea just popped out. I hadn't really thought about it, but it sounded good. I could work and learn at the same time, the way Mr. McCall did. I could write stories like Miss Harper Lee. I could dream, then try to catch the dreams on paper.

"My dream is a place," said Jarmaine. "Fisk University in Nashville, Tennessee."

"A college?"

"I want to do something with my life. Be a journalist or a lawyer like Thurgood Marshall."

"Who's he?" I asked.

She looked at me as if I'd stepped off a flying saucer. "*Brown versus the Board of Education*? The Supreme Court decision? 'Separate educational facilities are inherently unequal.' Thurgood Marshall was the lawyer. What do they teach you at your school?"

"Not that," I said.

"Things are happening at Fisk. There's a group called the Nashville Student Movement. They integrated the lunch counters last year. They met with the mayor, and he backed down. I'm going to join them."

"The mayor backed down? To some students?"

Jarmaine nodded. "Their leader is a woman, Diane Nash. She's a Fisk student. She led a demonstration at the capitol."

"You couldn't do that here," I said.

"The demonstration?"

"Any of it. Not in Alabama."

Jarmaine picked up a section from last week's paper that was folded next to her on the bench and pointed to a small article.

Negro Group Sets Bus Mixing Tour

WASHINGTON (UPI) – More than a dozen Negroes and whites planned to board buses today and head south to break the color barrier on Dixie's highways.

The travelers, picked and trained by the Congress of Racial Equality (CORE), will ride the commercial buses through Virginia, the Carolinas, Georgia, Alabama, and Mississippi.

So Lavender had been right. It really was happening.

"I heard about that," I said. "Your mother told me. She said they're called Freedom Riders."

Jarmaine nodded. "They've been trained in nonviolence, like Mahatma Gandhi. No matter what people do to them, they won't strike back. They started their trip last Thursday in Washington, DC, and plan to finish in New Orleans. They're coming through Anniston this Sunday. They're making history, and I'll be at the Greyhound station to see them."

"Does Lavender know you're going?" I asked.

"No," said Jarmaine, "and you're not telling her."

I shook my head quickly. "Don't worry. I won't."

Her eyes bored into me. She was strong, I could tell. But she was nervous. She was proud but not used to showing it.

I know because she blushed.

CHAPTER
NINE

Afterward, Jarmaine and I walked inside, where she went back to work. I found Grant leaning against his father's desk, fooling with his camera. We said good-bye to his dad and headed for our bikes. As we did, I noticed Gurnee Avenue just a block away. I reached for Grant's hand, squeezed hard, and dragged him up the street.

"Hey!" he croaked.

Halfway up Gurnee was a yellow-brick building with an awning and a sign: *Greyhound*. It was the Anniston bus station, where buses stopped before heading down the Birmingham Highway, and where Jarmaine planned to come on Sunday to see history being made.

Next to the building was an alley, and in the alley was a bus. Stopping in my tracks, I gazed at the bus.

Where was it going? Who would be on board? What did they dream of?

Beside me, Grant wrenched his hand free.

"Jeez," he muttered. "The grip of death."

"Poor baby," I said.

I approached the bus and saw that it was empty. Glancing around, I reached for the door. It was locked. Apparently the bus was between trips. I ran my fingers along the silver stripes under the windshield. For years I'd been watching buses drive past my house. It wasn't often that I got to see one up close. I wanted to remember what it looked like and how I felt standing beside it.

As I touched the bus, I saw a road, maybe the Birmingham Highway or one of the new interstates they were building. It curved out of sight, and I wondered what was at the other end—hope, happiness, questions, pain? Someday maybe I'd climb on the bus and find out.

Behind me, Grant asked, "What are you doing?"

I turned around to face him. "Take my picture."

"Here? Now?"

"Yes!"

He stifled a grin. "All I've got is color film. I hate to waste it."

I slugged him.

"Okay, okay."

The picture seemed important, not just because of what it showed but who took it. I was there. Grant was there. The bus was there. They were all pieces of my future, if I could just figure out how to put them together.

"Take it," I said.

He shrugged, took the camera from over his shoulder, and peered through the lens. "Say cheese."

"That's stupid," I said. "I've got a better word."

He lined up the shot.

"Freedom," I said.

Click. And it was done.

The bus station was just a block from Noble Avenue, where people in Anniston went to shop. It reminded me of something.

"You go on home," I told Grant as he carefully wiped the lens and put a cap over it. "There's something I need to do."

We said our good-byes, and I walked back toward the shopping district with one question on my mind.

What should I get Mama for Mother's Day?

I'd been thinking about it since Daddy had slipped me the money on Friday. I had scanned ads in the paper, but nothing seemed right.

Reaching Noble Avenue, I passed Havertys Furniture, Goold's Hat Shop, Clark's Credit Clothiers, and finally came to Wikle's Rexall Drugs, where they had a little bit of everything. I looked over the products but couldn't make up my mind. I almost bought some perfume but decided not to. Mama liked things that worked, things that had a function.

Next I tried Charlie's Lucky Shopping Center, then Mason's Self-Service Department Store. Finally, in a corner of Mason's, I found it. They had a big display of straw handbags, and I spotted one with a picture of a duck on the side. I was pretty sure Mama loved ducks, or was it peacocks? Anyway, this was something useful. It could be a present from Royal and me.

I grabbed the bag, then picked out Mother's Day cards from Royal, Daddy, and me. I went to the counter, where I took Daddy's five-dollar bill from my pocket and handed it to Mrs. Jutson, who had sold me my first Easter bonnet.

"It's for Mother's Day," I told her.

Mrs. Jutson nodded, smiling. "I'm sure your mama will be very happy. Please tell her hello for me."

"Yes'm, I will."

I left Mason's proud of myself, glancing at the bag and imagining what Mama would say. As I did, I bumped into someone.

"Oops! Excuse me," I said, looking up.

It was Jarmaine, carrying her schoolbooks.

"That's all right," she said. "I wasn't paying attention either. I was just going home."

"Finished for the day?"

"Not yet," she said. "I have to do some homework."

I thought of the times Lavender had helped me do my homework, while Jarmaine had been at home doing her own. It didn't seem right.

I said, "Hey, Mother's Day is coming up, right?"

Jarmaine nodded.

"I could help you pick out a present for Lavender."

"That's nice of you, Billie, but I already have one."

"Well, then, here's an idea. Maybe I could get her a present myself. After all, she takes care of me too. She's kind of like my mother."

I thought Jarmaine might smile. Instead she winced as if I had hit her.

"Are you okay?" I asked.

"I'm fine," she said.

I wondered how often Negroes in my town had said those words when they weren't fine at all. I wanted it to be different with Jarmaine and me.

"What's wrong?" I asked.

Jarmaine studied me. "You don't know, do you?"

"What? Tell me."

"She's not your mother. Hearing you call her that makes me feel bad."

I stepped back, surprised. Talking with Jarmaine was like walking on ice—you never knew when you might fall through and come up shivering.

"I'm sorry," I mumbled.

Reaching into my pocket, I felt the two dollars in change that Mrs. Jutson had handed me and thought I might be able to use it as a peace offering.

"You want a milk shake?" I asked. "We could get one at Wikle's."

She looked at me and shook her head. "Wake up, Billie. Look around. This is your street, not mine. I'm a Negro. I don't shop around here—look what happened to my friend Bradley. And Wikle's? If I sat at the lunch counter, they'd arrest me."

"For having a milk shake?"

"Welcome to Alabama."

Jarmaine lowered her gaze and started up the side-walk.

I called after her, "It shouldn't be like that."

She hugged the schoolbooks to her chest and kept going.

CHAPTER TEN

Darkness is your friend.

Daddy used to tell me that when I was little. I was afraid of the dark, like a lot of kids. So when Daddy came to my room to kiss me good night, I always begged him to stay. He would sit for a few minutes on the edge of the bed, holding my hand. When he got up to leave, he would say those words in a kind, gentle voice.

I began to believe him. I guess I still do. Darkness is mysterious. It's promising. You can wrap it around you like a shawl.

Grant had a room full of it, a darkroom.

I was thinking about it later that week when Grant and I rode to his house after school. Mrs. McCall must have seen us coming, because she pushed open the screen door and came out carrying two glasses of lemonade. She was tall like Grant, with a handsome face, pretty eyes, and a quiet manner.

She handed us each a glass of lemonade, then went back inside. The glasses were sweating. It reminded me of what Mama always said: "Horses sweat, men perspire, women glow." After bicycling home on a warm day, I was glowing like mad.

I took a gulp of the cold, delicious lemonade. It was the McCall family's favorite drink. Grant's mom bought lemons by the bushel basket from old Mr. Bell, who had a fruit stand down the street. You could smell the lemons whenever you were around the McCalls—clean, fresh, a family with zest.

A bicycle rider coasted down the hill, with a heavy bag hanging from his handlebars. It was Arthur the Arm, a neighborhood kid earning a few bucks as a paperboy before moving on to his true calling, star pitcher for the Detroit Tigers. He reached into the bag, grabbed a rolled-up newspaper, and sent it spinning toward the porch, where it landed with a plop in front of Grant.

"Nice shot," called Grant, and Arthur nodded.

Grant opened the paper and scanned the front page. He looked off into the distance, then down at his camera, which he was carrying with him as usual.

"I'm going to be a news photographer," he said.

"When did you decide this?" I asked.

"I guess I've always known. I'll tell stories with pictures, the way my father does with words. I'll show what's good and what's hurtful. I'll fight for justice. I'll make people think."

I imagined Grant at City Hall, snapping photos of the mayor, with his sleeves rolled up and a hat pushed back on his head. In the hat was a card that said *Press*. I had to admit, he looked good.

"Speaking of pictures," I said, "what about that other one?"

"Which one?"

"You know, me at the bus station. Could you develop it?"

"I suppose so. I need to do some work in the darkroom."

"Could I come with you?" I asked.

He shrugged. "If you want."

It was a little room at the back of the house where Grant developed and printed his photos. Grant's dad had helped him cover the window and any cracks around the door so no light would enter. When we went in, Grant switched on a lamp and showed me some equipment. On a table there were trays that he called baths and a large metal device attached to a pole, which was an enlarger.

Closing the door behind us, Grant turned off the lamp and flipped a switch, and the room turned red. He explained that you can use red light when developing black-and-white photos because it helps you see but doesn't hurt the pictures. I watched while he developed and printed some shots he had taken at school. The photographic paper was blank, but then pictures appeared like magic.

There was the school band. There was the principal, Mr. Stephens. There was Phil Carruthers, the student body president, and crouched behind him, giggling, was Lisa "Big Baby" Barnes, the class clown. The pictures were everyday scenes, but something about them was thrilling. I was seeing the world through Grant's eyes.

"What about the bus station?" I asked.

"That's different," said Grant. "I was shooting color."

"So?"

"I have to change the chemicals. And we can't use the red light—that's only for black and white. It would ruin color photos."

He spent a few minutes setting things up. Then he turned to me. "Ready?"

"I guess."

He turned off the light, and the room went away. It wasn't red. It wasn't any color at all. It was what you see when you close your eyes at night.

Darkness. Deep, deep darkness.

"This is how you develop color photos," he said.

How odd, I thought. *Red for black and white, black for color.*

I heard Grant rustling around next to me.

"What are you doing?" I asked.

"Working."

"How am I supposed to watch? I can't see."

Grant's hands touched mine and guided them around the table. "Here's a tray. Here's the enlarger. Here's the paper I'll print on."

His hands were warm. They seemed strong and sure. Maybe it was my imagination, but I thought they lingered a moment longer than they had to.

I wanted to ask, *What are you thinking? When you look into the darkness, what do you see?*

I heard rustling sounds again. Grant was doing what he loved. It was so much a part of him that he could do it blind. I wondered what it was like to be so sure of yourself.

A few minutes later he turned on the light.

"I made two of them," he said, "in case you want an extra."

On the table were twin pictures of me. My skin was pink. My hair was red. My eyes sparkled, and my grin flashed. Behind me, the Greyhound bus glinted silver and blue, ready to take me on a journey.

Grant picked up the photos and handed them to me. "These are yours."

I took them, then thought about it and handed one back.

"You keep this one," I said.

CHAPTER
ELEVEN

We always tried to make Mother's Day special.

Daddy and I woke up early that Sunday and tiptoed into the kitchen, where we made sausage and hockey pucks—I mean, pancakes. We were out of syrup, but there was an old jar of strawberry jam left in the back of the fridge, and we pulled that out. I picked some buttercups from the yard and put them in a pickle jar. Daddy woke up Royal and brought him into the kitchen. Then I set everything on a tray and led the way to Mama's room.

In the hallway I turned to Daddy and whispered, "Isn't there a song?"

"Huh?"

"For Mother's Day. You know, like 'Deck the Halls'

for Christmas, or 'Auld Lang Syne' for New Year's."

Daddy thought about it. "Not that I know of."

He held open the bedroom door, and I walked through, singing "Happy Mother's Day to you…"

Okay, it was weak. But Mama beamed anyway, like she was at the Ritz Carlton Hotel in New York City, where *Life* magazine said Miss Harper Lee liked to eat. I was just happy to see Mama smile.

Daddy got the Sunday paper, and after breakfast I sat next to Mama on the bed and read it with her while Daddy played with Royal on the floor. Mama and I went through the comics, of course, including my favorites, *Flash Gordon* and *Peanuts*. There was a cartoon saying "Every day is Mother's Day"—Mama liked that—and a sappy poem in the ad for Long's Funeral Home.

The sun shone on the bed. I rested my head on Mama's shoulder. Daddy ruffled Royal's hair. It was just the four of us in our own little world. Daddy winked at me. Royal laughed. Mama glowed. Sometimes I think it was the last good moment.

When we finished the comics, I slipped into the other room and brought back the straw handbag, which I'd wrapped in tissue paper the night before.

"Ducks!" said Mama when she tore it open. "I love ducks!"

"I thought you loved peacocks," said Daddy.

Mama hugged Royal and me; then Daddy presented his card and gift. The gift was so big he couldn't get it onto the bed. Mama had to open it on the floor. She ripped through several miles of ribbon and wrapping paper, and underneath found a giant cardboard box, which Daddy helped her open with his pocket knife.

"A vacuum cleaner!" said Mama finally. "How romantic."

Personally, I didn't think it was that romantic. Maybe Mama didn't either.

Daddy shrugged. "You've been talking about keeping the house clean. I thought this would help."

Mama flashed a stiff little smile. "Lavender will be thrilled."

* * *

Down the other side of our hill, toward town, was the Wayside Baptist Church, where we went on Sundays. It was a little brick building with a sign out front.

God couldn't be everywhere, so he made mothers.

It was another one of Pastor Bob's gems. There was a different message each week. Daddy said the guy spent more time on the sign than he did on his sermons.

That morning, Mama carried her Bible in the straw handbag. We took Royal to the nursery, then sat in our usual spot on the aisle five rows from the front, which I liked because you could see out the window. I watched Jimmy McReedy work on his motorcycle next door, revving the engine every so often and drowning out Pastor Bob. It was just as well, because the sermon was about Mary, the mother of Jesus. The problem was, I think Pastor Bob got her mixed up with another Mary. I have to say, though, I couldn't blame him. Let's face it—there are too many Marys in the Bible.

I lost track of the sermon and glanced at the people around me. I'd grown up with them. They seemed almost like family. There was Clyde of Clyde's Hair Heaven. A few rows behind him sat Mrs. Jutson, the clerk at Mason's. On the other side of the church I spotted Mr. Tolbert, the band director and my homeroom teacher. He caught my eye and smiled. Maybe his mind was wandering too.

Daddy had a saying: they aren't all good people, but they're our people. He meant the folks in town and around it, the ones he sold insurance to, the ones I'd grown up with and gone to church with and said hello to when I passed them on the street. They were part of me, like summer days and the honeysuckle in our yard. After what happened later that day, I often wondered if it was still true.

I looked around the church and realized that all the faces had one thing in common. They were white. That started me thinking about Jarmaine. If she walked through the door of our church, what would happen? Could she sit in the sanctuary the way she and her friends did at the spelling bee? What would Pastor Bob say? Would he preach about love like he was doing this morning?

I thought about Jarmaine's church, which probably was as black as mine was white. Were they also talking about Mary? Was their Mary white like ours? If she was black, did that mean Jesus was black?

Lavender didn't work on Sundays, so after church Mama started for the kitchen.

I told her, "It's Mother's Day. Daddy and I can make dinner."

She squeezed my shoulder. "That's all right, Billie. I'll take over now."

We had ham and biscuits, then boiled custard, which was like eggnog but better. Mama kissed Royal and told us how proud she was to be our mother and Daddy's wife.

Afterward, I washed the dishes and Daddy excused himself, saying he had an errand to run. Then I grabbed the Sunday paper, plopped down on the sofa next to

Mama and Royal, and looked through the sports section.

Reading the paper reminded me of the Freedom Riders, and I remembered this was the day they were coming through Anniston. I pictured Jarmaine at the Greyhound station and thought she must be excited.

They're making history, she had told me. Could it be true? How do you make history by riding on a bus? I'd been watching buses drive by for as long as I could remember. The people on them were going places. Were these riders different? Did they have dreams like I did? If you had a dream, could you make history?

I wanted to catch a glimpse of them and realized that I could. Jumping up from the sofa, I headed to my room, where I opened my drawer and got out the bus schedule. On Sundays, only one bus went from Atlanta to Birmingham, and according to the schedule, it had just arrived in Anniston. I allowed for some time to load passengers and figured the bus would be leaving the Greyhound station in a few minutes, which meant it would come through our neighborhood soon.

I called to Mama, "I'm going outside," then flew through the door and ran to Grant's house.

"Come with me," I told him. "Bring your camera."

We hopped on our bikes and raced down the hill

to Forsyth's Grocery, where the little dirt parking lot would give us the best view.

As we parked our bikes in front, Grant asked, "What's this all about?"

I was going to tell him, but at that moment the bus appeared at the top of the hill.

"Just start taking pictures," I said.

CHAPTER TWELVE

I could tell right away that something was wrong.

The bus weaved back and forth. As it drove down the hill, I saw dents on the side. I heard a rattling sound and then a *thump-thump*, *thump-thump*.

The strangest part was the cars and pickup trucks. A line of them followed the bus, snaking back all the way to the top of the hill and beyond.

"Hey, there's my dad!" said Grant, pointing.

I saw Mr. McCall's car, third in line.

"What's he doing?" I asked.

"Working on a story. He went downtown after lunch. He didn't say what it was, but I noticed he didn't call his photographer. I guess it didn't seem like a big enough story."

"I guess he was wrong," I said.

Grant glanced down at his camera. A look crossed his face—part happiness, part determination.

The bus drew near, and I saw what had caused the thumping. The tires were slashed and had gone flat. I knew the bus couldn't go much farther, and sure enough, right in front of the grocery, it pulled to the side of the road.

The door popped open, and the driver came stumbling out, with another man right behind him. They hurried across the parking lot and into the grocery, maybe to ask for help. I saw that the cars were pulling over too, parking every which way alongside the road.

Have you ever stumbled onto a wasps' nest? I did once when I was little. It was an accident, but the wasps didn't know that. They were mad.

That's what the people reminded me of. They swarmed out of their cars, carrying sticks and clubs and chains. One group gathered along the side of the bus and started rocking it back and forth, trying to turn it over.

Frightened, I reached back for Grant, but no one was there. I looked around, worried, then spotted him in the crowd. He was taking pictures. I saw Mr. McCall nearby, observing the crowd and scribbling in a little notebook. Father and son were both trying to under-stand in the ways they knew best.

I was trying to understand too. These were some of the same people I'd seen on the street and in the grocery store. I'd seen them in church that morning. I was part of them, and they were part of me. It was as if my right arm, without warning, had suddenly started punching.

There was a crash as a young man broke a bus win-dow with a metal crowbar. Next to him, a teenager gripped a baseball bat, maybe one he had used in a game on Saturday, and smashed another window.

When the group realized they couldn't turn over the bus, they started for the door, trying to get inside. A man stood in the opening. He was white and seemed to be a passenger. The group hesitated. The man ducked back in, pulling the door shut behind him. The crowd pounded on it, but apparently the man had locked it.

"You can't keep us out!" shouted the young man with the crowbar.

He broke out the rest of the window, then dropped his crowbar and tried to pull himself up through the jagged opening. Glass cut his hands, but he didn't stop. Someone reached out through the window and pushed him back. He growled like an animal. His friends gathered behind him, yelling threats—ten, then twenty, then fifty of them.

I had no doubt who they were threatening. On the other side of the window huddled the Freedom Riders, black and white people traveling together, people Jarmaine had said were trained not to strike back no matter what happened. I wondered if they had ever imagined anything like this.

Certainly I never had—not in my neighborhood, in front of Forsyth's Grocery, the store that carried Bunny Bread and baseball cards and all the latest records.

My gaze swept over the scene and up the hill, where the crowd had parked their cars. I saw a car I hadn't noticed before. It was a beat-up DeSoto, the one we had bought from our neighbors. Suddenly I got a terrible feeling in my stomach.

I scanned the crowd and realized for the first time that there were two groups—one beating on the bus and one watching. The watchers milled around, some of them shouting encouragement. Besides men, there were women and children, several still wearing their Sunday best. There was old Mrs. Todd, who shopped at Forsyth's Grocery. Beside her was Clyde of Clyde's Hair Heaven. One woman had a beautiful pink dress with a red carnation pinned to the front.

"Communists!" she yelled.

Next to her, a little boy picked up a stone and threw it at the bus.

That's when I saw Daddy.

He was speaking with Mr. Young, a man who lived down the street. Daddy talked and nodded, keeping his eyes fastened on the bus.

What did he see? What did he think? What would he do?

He glanced around, and his eyes met mine. He looked away, embarrassed, then looked up again. This time, his gaze, warm and steady, connected us like a cable. It was the gaze I'd grown up with, the one that had told me everything was all right. Except now it wasn't. The scene dropped away—the sound, the violence, the mob. There were just Daddy and me, like so many times before.

I caught a flash of white out of the corner of my eye and turned to see two highway patrol cars pull up at the edge of the parking lot. The doors opened, and the officers got out. They looked around, but instead of stopping the crowd they leaned against one of the cars, arms folded, sunglasses glinting. They watched, talking calmly to each other.

"Hey!" I yelled to them, waving my arms. They didn't see me.

I looked back at the crowd and recognized one man, Bo Blanchard. He was a member of the local Ku Klux Klan, a group that was against Negroes or anybody else who disagreed with them. The Klan and its members were supposed to be secret, but Bo Blanchard couldn't keep his mouth shut.

I saw him step away and sprint for his car, which was parked up the hill. A moment later he came running back to the bus, holding a bunch of oily rags. He pulled a lighter from his pocket and held it up to the rags. They burst into flames. He flung them through one of the broken windows.

There was a dull *whumpf.* Flames leaped. The bus was on fire.

CHAPTER THIRTEEN

The passengers screamed. One of them, a young Negro woman, leaned through a broken window, gasping for air.

She yelled, "Oh my God, they're trying to burn us up!"

The fire blazed behind her, and smoke began to billow. More passengers stuck their heads through the windows, their eyes wide with fright. I realized that the people in the bus had a terrible choice: face the flames inside or the mob outside.

Hearing desperation in the passengers' voices, the mob clustered around the door. One man smacked a lead pipe against his palm. Another broke a bottle and held it by the neck.

"Burn them alive!" cried one.

"Fry them!" called another.

Grant took pictures. The highway patrol officers just watched.

The smoke turned an inky black, the color of midnight. Suddenly there was an explosion. Flames leaped from under the back of the bus.

"The fuel tanks!" yelled one of the men. "They're gonna blow!"

The mob backed away. Some ran. The bus door flew open, and people spilled out in a jumble of black and white. Most ended up on their hands and knees, coughing and retching from the smoke.

A young white man approached one of the passengers and asked, "Are you okay?" Then he took out a baseball bat and swung it, smashing the passenger on the side of the head.

The mob hesitated. Some who had run away moved back toward the bus, carrying tire irons and chains, falling on the passengers and beating them.

Everyone watched, including me. I wanted to do something, but I couldn't move. Then I saw a small figure through the smoke. Janie Forsyth, who must have heard the commotion from inside the grocery, weaved in and out among the victims, carrying a bucket of water and a stack of Dixie cups. She dipped the cups in her bucket and fed sips of water to the passengers. Pausing under the S&H Green Stamps sign, she gave a handkerchief to one passenger, and he wiped blood from his face.

I wondered if she would get beaten too, but no one touched her. They knew her. She was the Forsyth girl. Maybe it was easier to beat up a stranger.

Another fuel tank exploded, sending flames to the sky and driving the last of the passengers from the bus. A moment later, it was a mass of red and black, burning like a bonfire. I could feel the heat all the way across the parking lot.

I heard the crack of a gunshot, then another. Fearing the worst, I whirled around. The highway patrol officers were standing nearby, pistols pointed to the sky.

"That's enough," one of them yelled.

Enough? What did the word mean? Grant had enough baseball cards. I had enough records. Was there enough blood? Enough pain?

The people in the crowd looked at each other. They eyed the passengers, who were scattered across the lot weeping, staring, stunned. Maybe they noticed Grant and realized he was taking photos. Whatever the reason, they moved off one by one, somehow no longer a mob. They went to their cars, got inside, and drove off.

They left in an orderly way, as if they'd just finished up at the grocery store.

The officers watched the cars go. They didn't write down names or license plate numbers. They didn't arrest anyone. One of them pulled a microphone from inside his patrol car and ordered an ambulance.

That seemed to break the spell. The second crowd, those who had been watching, began to move. Some left. A few approached the bus passengers and, along with Janie, did what they could to comfort the passengers until the ambulance arrived.

Daddy watched them go, the way he had watched the beatings and the flames. Finally he walked over to me. I thought of how, in an earlier life, he and I had made breakfast, then taken it in to Mama and celebrated Mother's Day.

I said in a low voice, "I guess now we know what your errand was."

"Clyde told me about it at the barber shop on Saturday," said Daddy. "I didn't know you'd be here."

"That was terrible," I said.

"It was dangerous. You shouldn't have come."

"Why did they do it?" I asked.

This time, "they" didn't mean Negroes. It meant the people of Anniston. It meant us.

"It wasn't supposed to be like this," said Daddy. "It got out of hand."

"But why? The Freedom Riders were on a bus, that's all."

Daddy explained in that soft, gentle voice of his, the one he used to reassure me. "Sweetheart, you know why. It was black and white together."

"Mama said black and white should be separated."

"She's right. It's better that way. Maybe this proves it."

It's what I had been taught in a thousand little ways—separate entrances, separate drinking fountains, separate ways of talking to people and looking at them. It had been passed to me, and I had taken it. But today, seeing what had happened in my town, I thought of Lavender's question: Would I pass it on?

* * *

At supper that night, Mama served roast beef. Afterward she brought out some apple pie. I took a bite, then pushed my plate away.

"I'm not hungry."

Mama studied me with a pinched, worried expression. After Daddy and I had gotten home, I'd gone to my room and a few minutes later had heard the two of them arguing. I couldn't hear the words, but I could tell Mama was angry. Happy Mother's Day.

Mama glanced at Daddy, then back at me. "Your father told me what happened. Do you want to talk about it?"

What was there to say? My town was different from the way I'd thought it was. Maybe my father was too.

"No, ma'am," I said.

I could see her struggle to find words. "Bo Blanchard and those other people...what they did was wrong. It was vicious and mean. But the Negroes—"

"Freedom Riders," I said. "They weren't all Negroes."

"Maybe they were a little bit wrong too."

"They just wanted to ride the bus."

"Sweetheart," said Mama, "this is the way we are. We've lived like this for a hundred years. Things are changing, but they take time."

"Let me ask you something," Daddy said in a quiet voice. "If the Freedom Riders hadn't come here, would anyone have gotten hurt?"

"Well, no," I said.

"Then don't you think they might share some of the blame?"

In the parking lot of Forsyth's Grocery I had seen something awful. Was it here too, in my house, at our table? There were no angry mobs, no fires or threats, no clubs or chains—just apple pie, two cups of coffee, and a glass of milk. We weren't burning buses or beating people up. We weren't doing anything. Maybe that was the problem.

CHAPTER
FOURTEEN

Everybody talked about it at school the next day. They called it "the burning bus," like it was a movie or TV show. They were excited, and all I could think about was the way the passengers had been stretched out on the ground, bleeding and moaning. I tried to explain, but no one wanted to listen.

"They got what they deserved," said one girl.

"I wasn't surprised," said another.

Someone else said, "We're good people. We just don't like to be pushed."

The words had a hollow ring, and I realized why. Kids were just repeating what their parents had said. I pictured dinner tables all around town where opinions were dished out like casserole.

The strange thing was that while the rest of us talked about it, the teachers didn't say anything. They acted as if nothing had happened. Turn to page forty-three. What's the value of x? Describe the Peloponnesian War. While they droned on, I thought about what I'd seen and heard.

The ambulance called by the officer had arrived as Daddy and I left. Grant, who stayed to watch, told me the driver refused to accept any Negroes at first, but finally the white riders convinced him, and he took the most seriously injured to Anniston Memorial Hospital.

Grant and his father followed the ambulance to the hospital, where the riders were given rooms and the situation calmed down for a while. But when the sun set, a crowd gathered outside the hospital. Things got ugly, and the Ku Klux Klan threatened to burn the place down. At that point, hospital staff asked the riders to leave. The riders called around desperately, trying to find someone who would take them.

Finally, in the middle of the night, a caravan of cars pulled in from a Negro church in Birmingham. The riders limped out of the hospital and, while the police held back the crowd, were helped into the cars and driven off into the darkness.

I learned something else from one of the boys at school. He told me the Klan had struck a deal with the police. The police, he said, had allowed the crowd fifteen minutes to do what they wanted to the bus passengers before stepping in. That would explain why the officers had leaned against the patrol car while the riders were beaten and the bus was burned.

While I was talking to the boy, Janie Forsyth walked by. The boy snorted and looked away. She continued down the hallway, and the others turned their backs to her.

"What are they doing?" I asked the boy.

"Sending a message," he said.

I rode home from school that day with Grant. When I told him how the students had treated Janie, he shook his head. "That's stupid. They just do whatever their parents do."

I thought about Mr. McCall moving through the crowd with his notepad, and Grant close behind with the camera.

"So do you," I said.

I pedaled on ahead of him, eager to get home and see the afternoon paper. When I arrived, it was on the front porch, courtesy of Arthur the Arm. I tore off the string and opened the paper. Reading the headline and seeing the pictures confirmed it: what seemed like a bad dream had really happened.

Mob Rocks, Burns Big Bus
In County Racial Incidents

ANNISTON – Racial mob violence that drew the nation's attention to Anniston Sunday saw a Greyhound bus burned and sent at least a dozen passengers to Memorial Hospital.

The article, written by Mr. McCall, went on to describe what had happened in front of Forsyth's Grocery. Next to the story were some of Grant's pictures.

"Congratulations," I shouted to Grant. "You made the paper."

He rode up behind me and looked over my shoulder. His father's front-page article was good, but what brought the scene to life were the photos. They told the story in a few terrible images.

Smoke billowed from the bus while the Freedom Riders sprawled on the ground outside. A highway patrol officer raised his pistol to warn the crowd. A fireman, too late to help, inspected the charred seats inside the bus. The ambulance driver tried to give first aid while one of the riders was carried off on a stretcher.

"Congratulations?" said Grant. "I wish it had never happened."

We sat on the front steps and read the other articles. There had been two groups of Freedom Riders, one on Greyhound and another on a Trailways bus. The Trailways group had made it through Anniston and as far as Birmingham, but an angry crowd waiting at the station had attacked the riders, some of whom were now in critical condition. There were photos, and one showed a group of men clubbing a rider until his face was a bloody mess. The men in the photo looked a lot like the people who had attacked the bus in our own neighborhood. The faces were different, but the looks of anger and fear were the same.

Grant spotted another article next to the photos. "Hey, listen to this," he said. "The FBI is investigating what happened. They're in town talking to the Klan. Some people are saying the FBI is here because of Robert Kennedy, the attorney general. You know what that means, don't you?"

"Not really."

"If Robert Kennedy's involved, then so is his brother, John F. Kennedy. The president knows what happened on our street!"

Grant pointed to an article. "They're even talking

about it in Russia, on Radio Moscow. They're using it as propaganda, saying what a bad place the United States is. They mentioned Anniston by name."

The thought of people in Moscow knowing about my town gave me the creeps.

A few minutes later, Grant's mom called him and he headed home. I looked down at the paper and saw the photos again. One of them showed the crowd, and I recognized Uncle Harvey Caldwell. His expression reminded me of that day at Forsyth's when I had told him about the Freedom Riders. It was the first he had heard of them. Maybe he told some friends and they had told others. Maybe it was all because of me. I'd been trying to push the thought away, but it kept coming back.

I gathered up the paper and went inside, where Lavender was feeding the baby. When I set the paper on the dining table, she glanced at it, and a look came over her face. Or rather, it was no look. Her face was blank, like she'd pulled a curtain across it.

I didn't know what to say. "I guess you heard what happened," I told her.

She nodded, then dipped a spoon into the little jar of baby food and fed it to Royal.

"I'm sorry," I said. "I think what they did was awful."

She took a towel from over her shoulder and dabbed his chin.

I watched her face, looking for signs of the Lavender I knew. "Aren't you going to say anything?"

She grunted. "Nothing to say."

I wanted to ask what Jarmaine had seen at the Greyhound station, but Lavender wasn't supposed to know Jarmaine had been there. For that matter, Lavender might not even realize I knew her daughter.

"I met Jarmaine," I said.

The curtain lifted for a moment. Lavender seemed nervous, and I wondered why.

I said, "I talked to her at the spelling bee. Then I went to see Mr. McCall at the *Anniston Star*, and she was there. I like her."

"She's a good girl," said Lavender.

"Is she at the paper today?"

"No."

"What does she do after school?" I asked. "Is she at home?"

Lavender nodded. "She's all alone."

There was something about the way she said it. I thought she'd been saying those words in her head for a long time, like the refrain to a sad song.

I said, "I wish you could be with her."

Lavender blinked, then dipped the spoon into the jar and fed Royal.

I sat with her a few more minutes, then went into the kitchen, where Mama kept Lavender's address and phone number taped to the side of the refrigerator. I copied the address on a scrap of paper, tucked it into my pocket, and headed out the door.

CHAPTER
FIFTEEN

The town of Anniston was really two towns.

There was the part I knew, with Wikle's Drugs, the *Anniston Star*, and Mason's Self-Service Department Store. Then there was another part, centered around the intersection of Fifteenth and Pine, where the faces were black.

I rode my bike down Fifteenth, passing Cobb Avenue High School, Golightly's Barber Shop, and Jubilation Car Repair. When I came to Pine Avenue, I stopped to rest. It was a warm day—"close," as Mama would say, which meant the wet, hot air pressed against you like a blanket. I looked around and saw low brick buildings. People drifted in and out, shopping and passing the time. A young mother with four children entered a big church building made of gray stones. The sign said *Miracle Revival Temple*.

According to the paper in my pocket, Lavender's house was just a few blocks farther, at 1605 Moore Avenue. When I turned onto that street, a woman with brown skin and gray hair stopped in her tracks and gaped at me as if she'd spotted some exotic bird. I smiled. She just stared.

The house, a white wooden bungalow with redbrick steps, was old but neat. I could see Lavender's touch on the front porch in a jar of pansies. She came to my house nearly every day, but I had never seen hers.

I parked my bike on the sidewalk, went up the steps, and knocked on the screen door. I heard footsteps, and Jarmaine appeared behind the screen, wearing a summer dress. When she saw me, her eyes opened wide.

"What are you doing here?" she asked.

"Visiting."

Jarmaine glanced up and down the street. "People might not like it. You know, after yesterday."

"That's what I wanted to talk about."

"There's nothing to say," she told me.

"Mr. McCall wrote about it. Did you see the paper?"

Jarmaine nodded.

I said, "You were at the bus station. What happened?"

She looked past me. I turned and saw the woman with gray hair watching us from the sidewalk.

Jarmaine pushed open the screen door, her face tense. "Come on in."

It was warm in the house. An electric fan turned from side to side, barely moving the air. It reminded me of the way our house had been before we got air-conditioning.

The living room was perfectly straight and clean. I got the feeling that, like my grandmother's living room, you only sat in there on Sundays or if somebody died. Beyond it was the dining room, where Jarmaine's notebook and papers were spread across the table. Her social studies book was battered and worn. I recognized it as one we had used at Wellborn before we got our new textbooks.

"I'm having a Dr. Pepper," said Jarmaine. "You like RC Cola, right?"

"Did your mom tell you that?"

"She tells me everything."

While Jarmaine disappeared into the kitchen, I took a minute to look around. I'd never been in Lavender's house, but I recognized a dozen details: the way she stacked coasters by the lamp, kept a folded quilt in the rocking chair, lined up family photos on the mantel.

Jarmaine returned from the kitchen and approached the table. She picked up two of the coasters and used them for the soft drink bottles. Then she settled into a chair, and I sat across from her.

I took a gulp of RC. It tasted good. Mostly, it tasted cold.

I said, "You told me you were going to the Greyhound station to see the Freedom Riders."

Jarmaine nodded. "I thought it would be exciting. It was awful."

She studied her bottle but I could tell she was seeing a very different scene. "When I got to the station, the first thing I noticed was the cars. They were parked up and down Gurnee Avenue like there was a concert or a festival. I had expected just a few people, but there was a whole crowd milling around the station. They were white, and they carried clubs and chains."

"Were there any Negroes?" I asked.

She shook her head. "Maybe they were still in church. Maybe they'd heard there would be trouble. Anyway, it was just me. I was scared, so I watched from across the street. When the bus turned the corner, the crowd started yelling. 'Go home!' 'Communist!' Things like that. Hateful things.

"The bus pulled up next to the station, and the crowd surrounded it. They beat on the side of the bus.

One man lay down in front to keep it from leaving, and another one slashed the tires with a knife. Somebody threw a rock and broke a window. I was across the street, but I could feel the hate. I wondered what it must be like inside the bus.

"About that time, the police got there. I can't imagine what took them so long. You know what they did? They joked with the crowd. Didn't arrest anybody. Told that man to get off the ground, then waved the bus on through. When it left, people ran for their cars and followed it out of town. There must have been thirty of them, like some kind of caravan."

"Did you see Mr. McCall?" I asked.

"I certainly did. He was in the middle of it all, watching and writing in his notebook. I would have talked to him, but I didn't know what the crowd would do."

Jarmaine looked up at me, then back at her Dr. Pepper. She lifted it and took a sip. I could see her hand shaking.

We sat there for a minute; then I told Jarmaine what I'd seen—how the caravan had come over the hill and the slashed tires had given out, and the crowd had finished the job they'd started at the station. When I described Janie Forsyth, Jarmaine perked up.

"You know what they're calling her, don't you? The Angel of Anniston."

Janie Forsyth, the unlikeliest hero. An angel who wore glasses and won spelling bees.

There was something I'd been trying to say. Thinking about Janie, it finally spilled out.

"I think it was my fault," I said.

"What was your fault?"

"The bus, the riot—I think I caused it."

"That's crazy," said Jarmaine.

"I told them about the Freedom Riders," I said.

Her eyes narrowed. "I don't understand. Who did you tell?"

I described the Tall Tales Club and my trip to Forsyth's with Lavender.

"The men were talking about what had happened at the grocery—you know, about your friend Bradley. They were being mean to Lavender. I wanted to do something, so I mentioned the Freedom Riders. I said they were coming to Anniston on Sunday. The men seemed surprised. I don't think they knew. I'm the one who told them. I did it."

Jarmaine didn't say anything. She was thinking.

I said, "Word travels fast. They probably told their friends. Somebody made a plan. It was my fault."

Jarmaine shook her head. "The Freedom Riders want people to know. That's the whole point. You helped them."

"I did?"

"You spread the word. What people did about it was their problem, not yours."

I helped the Freedom Riders. Maybe instead of feeling guilty, I should feel proud. Then I thought of Daddy, standing in the crowd with Uncle Harvey Caldwell. What would he say?

"What do we do now?" I asked Jarmaine.

"I wish I knew."

"My father was there," I said. I don't know why, but I had to tell her.

She stared at me. "In the crowd?"

"He didn't hurt anybody," I said quickly. "He was just watching."

Jarmaine looked past me, out the window. "You know what they say, don't you? All you need for evil to win is for good people to do nothing."

I pictured Daddy standing there with his arms crossed. The bus burned, and the riders got beat up and nearly killed. All the while, he just watched.

Then it hit me. "I did the same thing. I stood by and watched."

Jarmaine nodded. When she spoke, I could barely make out her words. "I did too. I saw the mob at the station, beating on the bus, yelling bad things. I didn't even cross the street. I was too scared."

Children shouted in the distance. Someone plucked a banjo. The fan creaked as it turned one way, then the other.

"You know what I think?" said Jarmaine. "There are two kinds of people in the world—the watchers and the riders. You and me? We're watchers."

"I want to be a rider," I said.

"So do I," said Jarmaine.

CHAPTER
SIXTEEN

It was Boat Day in social studies class. At least, that's what the kids called it.

Mr. Duffy, our teacher, had been talking all year about the Greeks and Romans and Mesopotamians. He had arrived at the Middle Ages in March. Gutenberg invented the printing press in April. The climax came in May, when Columbus sailed three boats to discover America, the event that all of world history had been leading up to.

Each year when his class studied that event, Mr. Duffy brought in his models of the *Niña*, the *Pinta*, and the *Santa Maria*, which he had constructed out of toothpicks when he was thirteen years old.

Boat Day.

Mr. Duffy was a short, balding man who loved history and tended to sweat. He paced back and forth at the front of the class, describing Columbus's ships and wiping his forehead with a handkerchief.

"Think of it, kids," he said, pointing to the models. "I did this when I was your age. You can accomplish great things—all of us can."

As Mr. Duffy gave us a guided tour of his boats, I sat in the back row, thinking of things I could accomplish and the courage it could take.

Someone giggled.

It was Arlene Nesbitt. She sat next to Bubba Jakes, and he was whispering to her.

Mr. Duffy stopped his presentation. "Mr. Jakes, is there something you'd like to tell us?"

"No, sir," he mumbled. "Sorry."

Arlene glanced over at Bubba. "I'll tell them."

Grinning, she looked around at the class. "We were just talking about the boats. We wondered if the Negroes sat in back."

The others laughed, and Mr. Duffy suppressed a smile. "Let's stay on the subject, shall we?"

It made me mad—not just their laughter but my response. I didn't want to sit quietly anymore.

"What is the subject?" I found myself asking.

Heads swiveled around. People stared at me.

I said, "It's history, right? Well, what about the history taking place right here?"

"Miss Sims—"

"Two days ago, something happened in our neighborhood. People all over the world are talking about it. And what are we doing? Looking at boats made out of toothpicks."

Nobody said anything. Shifting in her seat, Arlene looked nervously at Mr. Duffy. "I like the boats."

"Columbus discovered America, but what about now?" I asked. "What's it like to live here? What's it like to ride on a bus and sit in back?"

Around me, people shook their heads and whispered.

"Some of you disagree with the Freedom Riders," I said. "I'm not sure what I think myself. But you have to admit, they're brave. They don't watch or laugh. They do something. They won't stop. They're not going away."

Mr. Duffy got a funny expression on his face.

"Oh," he said, "but they already have."

I looked up, confused.

He said, "Didn't you hear? It was on the news this morning. The bus drivers refused to take them farther because it was too dangerous. So the Freedom Riders went to the airport and took a flight out of Birmingham.

Now they're in New Orleans. The rides are over."

I just sat there. I didn't know what to say.

Arlene said, "That's good, isn't it? The people are safe. The trouble's passed."

She was wrong. The world was a mess. Bad things happened, even in Anniston. Good people stood by and watched. Some of them laughed.

I wanted to be a rider, not a watcher. But the riders got scared and ran away. They weren't so brave after all. They were like the rest of us—drifting along, seeing problems but not really doing anything.

Mr. Duffy went back to his boats. I barely noticed. I was sinking into a deep hole. What was the use? Why bother? What good was hope? Why have dreams if you don't do anything about them?

The Freedom Riders had given up, and so had I.

* * *

A hole is a nice place to be. It's dark. It's warm and comfortable. You don't have to move or think or feel. You can't get hurt.

I stayed there all day and into the next. My body walked and talked and rode a bike. Things moved around me, but I didn't care. I was in the hole.

When I got home from school on Wednesday I went straight to my room. I had homework but didn't feel like doing it, so I looked through my record collection. I wasn't in the mood for an itsy-bitsy bikini or a hound dog. I wanted dark. I wanted sad. I found it in "Teen Angel," a song about a girl who gets run over by a train. At the end, her boyfriend moans, "Answer me, please." Like the boy in the song, I needed an answer, and I wasn't getting one.

I played the record thirty-seven times, then went out on the front porch and slumped in the swing, rocking back and forth, back and forth. After a few minutes Grant came pedaling up the driveway, dumped his bike, and hurried over.

"Billie!" said Grant.

He peered into the hole from far away, his head the size of a BB.

"I've got the paper," he said breathlessly. "You need to see it."

"You've always got the paper. Why don't you just staple it to your forehead?"

"There's an article about the Freedom Riders!"

I closed my eyes and sighed. "They're done. It's over."

"That's just it," he exclaimed. "It's not over."

He held the paper up so I could see it. The article, just a headline and one sentence, was tucked in a corner of the front page.

BULLETIN

BIRMINGHAM (UPI) – A group of Negroes from Nashville, Tenn., attempted to resume anti-integration protests today at the Birmingham Greyhound bus terminal but police would not let them get off.

The word "Nashville" sent an electric charge up my spine. The corpse sputtered to life.

Grant said, "My dad's at his office, trying to get more information. He's working on a story."

Someone else was working on it too, I was sure.

"We need to find out," I said. "Come on!"

We raced to the phone, and I dialed the *Star*. Jarmaine was there, just as I had hoped. Grant leaned in so he could hear.

"Is it true?" I asked her. "Are the Nashville students coming?"

"They took a bus to Birmingham to continue the ride," she said, breathless. "They got there this morning, ten of them."

"Is Diane Nash with them?" I asked, remembering their leader.

"Mr. McCall says she's in Nashville running things.

He's been on the phone with her. But there was trouble. Bull Connor, head of the Birmingham police, wouldn't let the students off the bus. When they finally got out, he arrested them and took them to the city jail. That's where they are now—in jail, singing freedom songs."

There was pride in her voice and determination. I tried to imagine what it must be like in jail. If I had been there, I didn't think I'd be singing.

"What's going to happen?" asked Grant.

"They'll keep the Freedom Rides going," said Jarmaine. "And this time, no one will stop them."

Over the next two days, Grant and I followed the new Freedom Riders. Through phone calls with Jarmaine, we learned that the riders had stayed in jail all day Thursday. Then, in the middle of the night, Bull Connor woke them up, herded them into cars, and drove them off into the darkness. No one had seen them since.

Friday after supper, I called Jarmaine and asked, "Where do you think they are?"

Her voice sounded choked off and distant. "Have you heard of Billie Holiday?"

"Billie? Like me?"

"That's right. She was a singer. Died a couple of years ago. They called her Lady Day. We have some of her records. She had the most amazing voice. So beautiful. So sad. She was a drug addict. People mistreated her. You could hear the pain in her songs."

"I'd like to hear them sometime," I said.

"There's one song called 'Strange Fruit.' I can't sing it, but I know the words:

"Southern trees bear a strange fruit,
"Blood on the leaves and blood at the root,
"Black bodies swinging in the southern breeze,
"Strange fruit hanging from the poplar trees."

"I don't understand," I said.

"I think you do," said Jarmaine.

My mind, groping for an answer, slammed up against a wall. The wall was tall and wide. I think it had always been there. On this side of the wall we smiled and prayed and helped each other. We were nice. And on the other side? I tried to imagine what was there. It was dark and mean. It was filled with shadows. People whispered about it. I didn't dare look.

Jarmaine said, "You've heard the stories. I know you have. A mother is hungry and steals something. A man speaks disrespectfully. He looks at a white woman the wrong way. Then, late at night, they disappear. Someone finds them a few days later, hanging from a tree. Strange fruit."

I shivered. "You mean lynching? It really happens?"

"If you grew up the way I did, you wouldn't ask that question."

"You think the Freedom Riders might have been lynched?"

She said, "They disappeared in the middle of the night. This is Alabama. What do you think?"

Alabama. To me, it meant football. The Crimson Tide. Coach Bear Bryant. It meant my town and my neighborhood, places I loved. But for Jarmaine, the word was different. It scared her, I could tell. How could two people live in the same place and see such different things?

When I got off the phone I went to the window. The neighborhood looked calm, like it did every Friday evening. Next door, Grant and his parents sat on the porch, talking and sipping lemonade. The crickets chirped. The wind blew and the trees swayed.

Just another night in Alabama.

CHAPTER
SEVENTEEN

I went to my room and lay down. Closing my eyes, I saw the Freedom Riders dangling from trees. Nearby was the burned-out shell of a bus.

I guess I fell asleep, because when I woke up, the room was cool and someone had put a blanket over me. I glanced at the clock. It was after midnight. I pulled the blanket around my shoulders and went to the window. The McCalls' house was dark. Somewhere, in another dark place, Bull Connor was dealing with the Freedom Riders.

My mouth was dry, so I headed for the kitchen and got some water. I needed something to do. Remembering Daddy's words, I turned on the light, drew some water in the sink, and washed the dishes. It would help Mama, but it would also take my mind off strange fruit.

When I finished, I switched off the light and padded back down the darkened hallway, passing the little table where we kept our phone. It was all I could do to keep from lifting the receiver and calling Grant. Maybe he knew what had happened to the Freedom Riders.

I stared at the phone. Finally I took it off the table and, leaning against the wall, slid down to the floor. I cradled the phone against me and rocked it gently.

* * *

"Billie?"

I opened my eyes. Sunlight streamed through the window. Mama stood over me, clutching her bathrobe around her.

"Did you spend the night here?" she asked.

"I guess so," I mumbled.

"Silly girl."

She leaned over and kissed my forehead, then went back to her room to get dressed.

I thought of the Freedom Riders, and suddenly I was wide-awake. Bracing the phone against my legs, I picked up the receiver and dialed the McCalls' house.

There was a click, and Grant's mom answered.

I said, "Hey, Mrs. M., is Grant there?"

"Hi, Billie. He and his dad are at the office. They went early this morning."

"On Saturday?" I asked.

"Yes," she said. "It was something about the Freedom Riders."

"Thanks," I said and hung up.

I had scribbled Mr. McCall's work number on a pad by the phone. I started to reach for it, then changed my mind. I jumped to my feet, put the phone back, and hurried to my room. I threw on jeans and a T-shirt, then ran my fingers through my hair and hurried down the hall. Mama was just coming out of the bedroom.

"Have to go," I said.

"Billie—"

The screen door slammed. I was out the door and on my bike, pedaling for town.

* * *

As it turned out, it was a good thing I didn't telephone Mr. McCall, because I probably wouldn't have gotten through. When I arrived at the *Star*, he was on the phone. So were Grant and Jarmaine. As soon as they finished one call, they would hang up and dial another.

Mr. McCall saw me, nodded, and kept right on talking. "How many? Are they still in Birmingham?"

He took notes on a pad. "Uh-huh. Bull Connor? Right. So, what'll he do? Yeah, I'll believe that when I see it. Kennedy? Really? Okay. Keep me posted, huh?"

He hung up and started to dial again.

"What happened?" I asked him.

He kept dialing. It was Jarmaine, just finishing a call of her own, who answered my question.

"They came back," she told me.

I said, "The Freedom Riders? I thought Bull Connor was going to…you know."

Jarmaine shook her head. "It turns out that when he took them from jail Thursday night, he didn't hurt them. He just drove them to the Tennessee state line and dropped them off, luggage and all. Middle of the night, middle of nowhere. He told them, 'There's the Tennessee line. Cross it, and save this state and your-selves a lot of trouble.'"

I pictured the scene and tried to imagine how the riders must have felt, miles from home, with no idea where they were or what would happen.

"What did they do?" I asked.

"They gathered up their bags, found a phone, and called Diane Nash."

"So they went home?"

She looked at me like I was crazy. "Home? Lord, no. She sent cars to pick them up, and they rode back to Birmingham."

"Really? They're in Birmingham?"

"They *were* in Birmingham."

Grant, off the phone, chimed in. "They left. They're riding on!"

Mr. McCall, who had just hung up, saw the look of confusion on my face. "There were twenty-one of them, including eleven more from Nashville. They decided to catch the first bus from Birmingham to Montgomery, but when they got to the station, there was an angry crowd, and the drivers refused to go. That's when Robert Kennedy got busy."

"You know, the attorney general," said Grant. "The president's brother."

Mr. McCall nodded. "He was on the phone for hours, talking to the governor and the head of Greyhound. Kennedy threatened to bring in federal troops, and finally they made a deal. Greyhound would drive them, and the highway patrol would protect them. Early this morning, before the mob could gather again, the riders got on a bus and headed for Montgomery with a police escort."

The phone rang, and Mr. McCall picked it up.

I turned to Jarmaine. "So they're all right?"

"I hope so."

Next to her, Mr. McCall said, "What!"

He tucked the receiver under his chin, grabbed a

pad, and began taking notes. "Uh-huh. Right. Oh my God."

Grant and Jarmaine glanced at each other.

Mr. McCall scribbled. We waited. Finally, he replaced the receiver and looked up at us. His face was pale.

"There was a riot in Montgomery," he said, and referred to his notes. "A crowd was waiting for the bus, and they attacked the riders as they got off. Men had pipes and chains, women swung their purses, and children scratched with their fingernails. Meanwhile the cops were off to the side, calmly directing traffic. Twenty people were hurt, some seriously. A few are unconscious."

"Is the riot over?" asked Jarmaine in a small voice.

"Seems to be," said Mr. McCall. "The riders were taken to the hospital. The crowd gathered up the suitcases and built a bonfire in front of the bus station."

Jarmaine stood motionless, her expression stony. Tears ran down her cheeks. Grant put a hand on her shoulder.

She said, "How can people do that?"

Mr. McCall shook his head sadly. "I don't understand. I truly don't."

"You think the riders will keep going?" I asked.

Jarmaine blinked, and her expression changed. She gazed at me, her eyes flashing.

"They won't stop now," she declared.

"There's a mass meeting tomorrow night at First Baptist Church in Montgomery, to show support for the Freedom Riders," said Mr. McCall. "The riders will be there. So will the Negro leaders. Martin Luther King is coming in from Atlanta."

Jarmaine said, "Dr. King? Really?"

"Isn't he a preacher?" I asked.

"Dr. King is more than just a preacher," Grant told me. "He leads protests, like the Montgomery bus boycott. He's an activist."

The way Grant said the word made it sound like an honor. I'd heard Uncle Harvey Caldwell talk about Martin Luther King, but when Uncle Harvey called him an activist, it sounded different.

"Are you planning to write this up for the paper?" I asked Mr. McCall.

"You bet," he said, flipping through his notepad, "but I need more information."

He turned to Jarmaine. "We'll put a news flash in this afternoon's paper. Then, once we've got all the facts, I'll do an article for the Sunday edition."

Mr. McCall went back to his desk, pulled out a sheet of paper, and fed it into his typewriter. Grant reached for the phone. Jarmaine headed to the door, and I followed.

She took a seat out front, on the bench where I'd found her that first day. That had been less than two weeks ago, but it seemed like another lifetime in a different town, a place where people were kind and wouldn't hurt you. Thinking back on it, I wondered if that town had ever existed.

I sat down next to Jarmaine. She opened a brown paper bag, pulled out some peanut-butter crackers, and offered me one. She ate one herself, looking over the trees toward Montgomery, where the riders were healing and getting ready to continue their trip to New Orleans.

"I'm going," she said.

"Huh? Where?"

She turned and gazed at me. "To First Baptist Church. To the meeting. To see the Freedom Riders and hear Dr. King."

"For the newspaper?" I asked.

"For me."

I said, "Will your mother let you?"

"I'll leave early tomorrow morning. By the time she finds out, I'll be gone."

I bit into the cracker. "It's a long way to Montgomery. If your mother doesn't drive you, how will you get there?"

Jarmaine shrugged. "I'll take the bus."

CHAPTER EIGHTEEN

That stupid rooster.

He woke up at sunrise every morning, which was fine during the week. On weekends, though, I liked to sleep late—or as late as Mama would let me before rousting me out of bed to help with breakfast.

When the rooster crowed that morning, I remembered it was Sunday. I lay in bed staring at the ceiling. It was pink and orange, the color of the horizon.

In an hour or so, Mama would come in. We'd go to the kitchen and make Daddy's favorite coffee cake. Then all of us would dress up and go to church, where Pastor Bob would pray about loving our neighbors.

I loved my neighbors. I loved my town. But how far did love go? Did it stretch to Fifteenth and Pine where Jarmaine lived? Did it stretch to Birmingham or Montgomery?

Maybe love wasn't the answer. If you asked the Freedom Riders, they might say they just wanted respect. *Ignore me, even hate me, but let me live. Give me a chance.* Surely people could understand that. Somehow, though, my town didn't.

I had spent my life watching. When you watch, you notice. You think. You get restless. I wanted to do something.

Reaching over to the nightstand, I opened the drawer and took out the bus schedule. The Birmingham bus was leaving at nine fourteen, and Jarmaine would be on it. From there she would connect to Montgomery, where she would arrive by midafternoon. The trip wasn't long, but if you were by yourself, it might seem like an eternity.

It might go faster if you were with a friend.

The thought popped into my head like the flash on Grant's camera, freezing the action and lighting up the shadows. For as long as I could remember, I had watched the bus drive by my house. I had dreamed that someday I'd get on it and leave. I would go anywhere and do whatever I wanted. I would have perfect freedom.

Jarmaine wanted freedom, but it wasn't a dream and it wasn't perfect. It was something to fight for. It was a seat on the bus, and I could help her get it.

If I asked permission, Mama and Daddy would say no. Sometimes, though, you don't ask. You just do it, because you have to.

I put away the bus schedule and went to the window. The sky had turned bright red, flooding the yard with color. A nuthatch sang, and a pair of downy woodpeckers tapped on a tree trunk.

The day was just beginning. It could be any old Sunday, or it could be special. I took a deep breath. I looked off in the distance toward Montgomery.

I was tired of watching. I wanted to be a rider.

* * *

I found Jarmaine in front of the Greyhound station, sitting on the curb with a basket next to her. She had seemed so strong the day before, when she had talked about her plans. She seemed smaller now, like a young child.

I thought of a day at the state fair when I was seven years old and wanted to go on the Rotor. It was a giant cylinder where people would file inside and stand against the wall. When the ride started, the cylinder would tilt, then spin faster and faster. The floor would fall away, and the people inside would be pinned against the wall, staring down into blackness, held up by the laws of physics and nothing more. They screamed their guts out. It frightened me, but something about it was thrilling.

Daddy had seen me watching, my hands and face sticky with cotton candy.

"Are you scared?" he asked.

"I could never do that."

"It seems impossible," he told me, "but thousands of people do it every year. You know how?"

He looked down at me with a sweet smile on his face.

"They take one step, then another, then another. Before they know it, they're inside, whirling around and having the time of their lives."

I rode the Rotor that day. Daddy was beside me, screaming his guts out, grinning, and holding my hand.

Today Daddy was across town, sleeping next to Mama. I knew because I had peeked through the doorway and seen them. I had gone to my room and taken some allowance money from the top drawer of my dresser. Then I'd put on a dress, tiptoed to the kitchen, and gulped down some orange juice. I'd written a note telling them I was fine and would be back soon, but I hadn't said where I was going. I'd propped the note up on the counter and slipped out the door, feeling like a thief.

"Hey," I said to Jarmaine.

She looked up from the curb, startled.

"Want to take a trip?" I asked.

"You're going?"

"I think so. I'm scared."

"So am I," said Jarmaine.

She glanced over her shoulder at the station, a little brick building with an awning on the front and an alley on the side where the buses pulled in and out.

She said, "My mother wouldn't do this. My grandmother wouldn't. My grandmother's grandmother couldn't."

"Couldn't?" I asked. "Why not?"

"She was a slave."

The word hit me like a slap across the face. Jarmaine's great-great-grandmother, maybe very much like Jarmaine herself, had lived in a world where you could be bought and sold like a sack of potatoes. I thought of what I had learned in history class and realized that Jarmaine's idea of American history must be very different from mine.

Jarmaine straightened her shoulders. "I've decided to use the front door."

"Okay," I said.

She studied my face. "You don't understand. The colored door is around the side, on the alley."

I'd seen the signs all my life at the bus station, in parks, at the movies: *Colored Only.* The signs were posted over doors and restrooms and drinking fountains. I'd never thought much about them. They were part of the landscape, like sidewalks and traffic lights. At the city pool, there was even a day called "colored only," when, once a month, Negroes were allowed to swim there. The next day, the pool was drained, then filled up again so white people could use it.

I didn't think about the signs, but Jarmaine had to. When she went to the bus station, she couldn't go through the front door. Neither could Lavender or anyone else who shopped at Fifteenth and Pine. If Jarmaine walked through that door, she would be breaking the law.

"I was planning to do it last Sunday," said Jarmaine, "but instead I stood across the street. The mob rocked the bus and dented it with pipes. They broke the windows and slashed the tires. The riders could have been killed, and I didn't even go through the front door."

I thought of the times I'd walked through the front door of a store or the library or city hall. I'd never stopped to think about the people who couldn't, or how it made them feel. I'd just walked on through like I owned the place. In a way, I did. It was given to me, and to all the other white babies, on the day I was born. Meanwhile, across town, another group of babies was born. Their parents worked and bought homes and paid taxes like mine, but they didn't own the place.

It was my town. But it was Jarmaine's too, wasn't it?

Each day I did a thousand little things without thinking, while Jarmaine and her friends had to think and weigh and decide. If they didn't, they could get into trouble. They could be hurt. They could end up like the song. Strange fruit.

I stood there in front of the bus station and imagined the town of Anniston spread out before me, split in two. White only and colored only. Us and them. Safe and scared. I had lived my life in the safe part, ignoring the rest. When bad things happened, I didn't notice. When the bus burned, I stood to the side and watched.

What would happen if I stepped out of the safe part? Would I be scared? Would I be hurt? If I was, what would I do?

I'd been asking questions my whole life. It was time to get some answers.

"You can go through the front door," I told Jarmaine. "We'll do it together. Then we'll go to Montgomery."

She eyed me, weighing my words.

"It might be a hard trip," she said.

"I think we can do it."

Jarmaine climbed to her feet and brushed off her dress. She picked up the basket, then turned to me.

"Let's go," she said.

I fell in beside her. We took one step, then another, then another.

PART TWO

THE BELL

CHAPTER NINETEEN

No one noticed.

We went through the front door, and no one said a thing. Maybe it was because the place was almost empty, or because the Greyhound workers were busy.

I looked over at Jarmaine. She was blinking, and there were beads of sweat on her forehead.

"It's fine," I said.

She glanced around. "When I was little, my mother told me the rules. Now I'm breaking them."

We went to the ticket window. A middle-aged man looked out at me.

I said, "Montgomery, going through Birmingham. Two, please."

The man's gaze slid over to Jarmaine, then back to

me. He started to say something, then shook his head.

He told me the price. I paid my part out of the money I'd taken from my dresser. Jarmaine opened her purse and paid her part, and we took our tickets.

The man glanced at his watch, then up at me. He ignored Jarmaine.

"It'll be the next bus," he said. "Twenty minutes or so."

I thanked him, and when I turned around, Jarmaine was headed for the door to the alley, where the bus would come. I followed her outside.

"We could wait inside," I told her.

"I like it out here," she said.

Over her shoulder I noticed a sign on the side of the building: *Colored Waiting Area*. There were no chairs or vending machines, just an alley. I wondered if Jarmaine really did like it, or if she was just used to it.

We stood and waited. The heat rose from the black-top. I looked down the alley to the place where Grant had taken my picture, and I wondered what he was doing. I knew he wasn't in church because his family didn't go. Whenever I asked him what his religion was, he always said the same thing: justice.

"Are you sure you don't want to go inside?" I asked Jarmaine.

"Not this time," she said. "That's something else my mother told me. Choose your battles."

Finally the bus pulled into the alley. The door swung open, and an elderly white woman struggled down the steps. Behind her, the driver sprang to his feet and grasped her elbow.

"Careful there, ma'am," he said.

Jarmaine stepped forward and took the woman's hand, guiding her down the rest of the way. At the bottom, the woman smiled.

"Thank you, dear."

The driver followed the woman down and got her suitcase from the luggage compartment. Then we gave him our tickets and climbed the steps.

There were just a few people on the bus—a young white family with a boy and a girl sitting next to the windows on one side, two old white men off to themselves, and a middle-aged Negro woman in the last row. Jarmaine moved toward the family, then hesitated. She was looking at a row halfway back, just staring at it, as if some detail might suddenly pop up to let her know it was all right to sit there.

I wondered how long she had thought about doing this. The whole thing seemed strange. To me, it was just a bus. It was just a seat. To Jarmaine, though, it was a lot more, and today I was seeing it through her eyes.

Jarmaine took a deep breath and slid into the row. Behind me, the bus driver cleared his throat. Jarmaine studied her hands.

"She's with me," I said and slipped in next to her.

Jarmaine leaned over and whispered, "You don't have to sit with me."

The driver, arms crossed, gazed at us for a long time. Maybe he thought about the way Jarmaine had helped the old woman. Whatever it was, he turned and took his place in the driver's seat. He pulled a lever, and the door swung shut.

I pictured what it must have been like last Sunday— the Freedom Riders huddled inside; the mob outside, pounding on the bus; people screaming terrible things, their faces filled with hate. A few weeks ago such a scene would have been hard to imagine. Now, a week after Mother's Day, it was easy.

The bus pulled out of the alley and into the street. We were on our way.

We took Gurnee Avenue south, past the *Star* building to Eighth Street. Everything we saw was familiar to me. I'd seen it a hundred times on my bike and from the car when I came downtown with Mama and Daddy, but it looked different from a bus. Maybe it was the high angle, or knowing that others on the bus might never have seen it before.

Across from us, the young mother was looking out the window. She probably thought that Anniston was a nice town. In the last row, the Negro woman looked out the window too. I wondered what she thought.

We turned right on Eighth and headed west, out of town. At the city limits, Eighth Street became the Birmingham Highway, the two-lane road where I lived. I saw West Anniston Park, where I used to play on the swing set, and the little green house at the corner of Marshall Street where my friend Alice Cole lived. Wayside Baptist Church came up on the right. I saw from the sign that Pastor Bob had been busy again:

Shouting "Oh God!" does not constitute going to church.

A few minutes later we topped a hill, and there was Grant's house, with mine just beyond. A jolt went through me when I saw Mama and Daddy in our front yard, talking with Grant and his parents. Daddy looked worried. Mama looked sad. Seeing them, it was all I could do to keep from telling the driver to stop. As we rumbled by, Grant glanced up at the bus, then watched as we drove down the hill.

Forsyth's Grocery was at the bottom. There was a blackened area in the parking lot made by the smoke of the burning bus. Next door was the little house where the Forsyths lived. Maybe Janie was inside, practicing for the national spelling bee. I wondered if spelling would ever again seem important to her.

"That's where it happened, isn't it? Right there at the grocery."

Looking around, I saw Jarmaine gazing out the window. I nodded.

"I thought it would be bigger," she said.

As we rode on, the store receded. Then we turned a corner and it was gone.

Jarmaine lifted the basket she'd been carrying and set it on her lap. Inside, wrapped neatly in waxed paper, were pieces of fried chicken, some deviled eggs, and pie.

"Why did you bring food?" I asked.

"We always bring food on the bus," Jarmaine told me.

She glanced at me to see if I understood. I thought about the lunch counter at Wikle's Drugs, where Jarmaine wasn't allowed to eat, and I realized the Greyhound lunch counters would be the same. There were different rules for Negroes. The rules had been there all along, but I'd never thought much about them.

I looked into the basket, and suddenly I was starved. Jarmaine shared the chicken with me, and I recognized Lavender's recipe, which included a beautiful brown crust and lots of salt. I watched the other passengers while we ate. Jarmaine did too.

She leaned over to me and whispered, "They've barely even noticed us. I thought they'd be upset."

It might sound funny, but I was almost disappointed. The Freedom Riders had faced a mob. All we got was a couple of old men and a family.

I didn't know it then, but I should have remembered what Mama always said.

Be careful what you wish for.

CHAPTER
TWENTY

The bus sailed along, rocking gently from side to side. Instead of driving on the road, we seemed to float above it, like one of those ocean liners you see in the movies.

We passed through the town of Bynum. Wellborn High played them in football, and my family and I had driven there for some of the games. At Eastaboga, a little farther along, the Birmingham Highway ended, and we turned onto Route 78.

I liked being up high. You could see things. We swooped past houses, among rows of pine trees, and over rolling hills. I spotted a horse farm, a junkyard, and a deer processing plant. There were lots of churches. Some had signs but none were as good as Pastor Bob's.

We passed the road to Talladega and the little town

of Lincoln, then rode a bridge over the Coosa River. Downstream, just out of sight, was a place where Daddy had taken me fishing. Across the bridge were a beauty parlor and a field of rusted-out cars. We got stuck behind a logging truck. I looked up to see a flock of birds shifting like a cloud.

Somewhere past Harrisburg, the two old men on the bus started watching us. When I gazed back at them they looked away, but a few minutes later they were watching again. One had a sour expression on his face. The other just seemed curious. Every once in a while the sour one would mutter something to his friend.

Jarmaine saw them too. I realized she must always be on guard, studying people's faces. I had a feeling she'd been doing it her whole life.

Soon the old men were watching us more openly. The parents noticed and stared at us too. The mother glanced at the last row, where the Negro woman sat with downcast eyes, then back at us. I looked at the passengers and they stared right back, like we were animals at the zoo.

I noticed that the bus was quiet. Silence had settled over it like a dirty yellow fog. The tires hummed. I heard myself breathing. Next to me, Jarmaine shifted in her seat, trying to get comfortable and knowing it wouldn't happen.

A feeling rose up inside me. I wanted to say to them, "Is something wrong? Is my hair messed up? Is my dress crooked? Is there food on my chin?"

I clenched my fists, and Jarmaine must have noticed. She put her hand on my arm, but it didn't stop the voice inside my head.

"You want us to sit in back?" said the voice. "You want to kick us off? Maybe you want to burn the bus."

Jarmaine squeezed harder. The little girl played with her doll while her parents watched us. The doll reminded me of one I'd gotten when I was younger, during a brief frilly phase between football games. The little girl looked familiar. In fact, she could have been me. Her parents could have been mine.

They were just watching. It seemed harmless, but I saw now that it was a weapon. Watching can hurt. It can be painful, even if you don't lift a finger. It has weight. I felt it now, heavy against me, pushing us back, enforcing the rules. I had used it myself without even knowing it.

The passengers watched. The little girl played. The bus rode on, bound for Birmingham.

* * *

We came in next to the railroad tracks, in the poor part of town. There were shacks and shanties, places that made Jarmaine's house look like a palace. Children played in yards that were mostly dirt. They looked up when they heard the bus coming, the way I did at home. Here and there people were dressed for church, like flowers growing through the pavement.

We turned downtown and passed the Trailways station. I remembered how, on Mother's Day, a second group of Freedom Riders had taken a Trailways bus through Anniston and made it as far as Birmingham, to this station, where they were attacked and beaten by an angry crowd. I'd seen photos of it in the paper, but today I had trouble putting those pictures together with the neat building on that quiet city street.

The Greyhound station, just up the road, was a low structure that took up most of the block. This was where, after the riot, the original Freedom Riders had decided to stop. It was where the Nashville students, when they came on Wednesday to continue the ride, had been arrested and taken off to jail. They had been dumped at the border Thursday night and had come back to the station on Friday, but the buses wouldn't take them. Finally, with a police escort, a bus had driven them out of town just yesterday morning. The convoy must have come right down the road we were on, sirens sounding and lights flashing, headed off to meet a mob in Montgomery.

Our bus pulled into the loading area behind the station. The driver opened the door, and people gathered their things to get off. All Jarmaine and I had was her basket, so we were first down the aisle. The little girl stared as we walked by.

"Have a good trip," I told her.

The driver gazed at us. I took a deep breath. Then we stepped off the bus and into Birmingham.

CHAPTER
TWENTY-ONE

The lobby had a high ceiling that was lined with wood. Along the front entrance, windows stretched the full height of the building, and the morning light streamed in. On the floor were rows of wooden seats, like church pews. The ticket counter, baggage claim, and telephones lined the walls. Through a doorway to the left, I saw the restaurant that Jarmaine couldn't use. A security guard was stationed by the door, the only sign that there had been trouble. Workers, all of them white, stood behind the counters. A Negro custodian swept the floor and dusted the seats.

I checked the big clock above the ticket counter. It was almost eleven. The Montgomery bus was scheduled to leave at eleven thirty, so we had a half hour to wait. Without thinking, I sat in the white waiting area. Jarmaine hung back, eyeing a section in the corner marked *Colored Only*, where a well-dressed group of men, women, and children were crowded.

"Sorry," I said, getting to my feet.

I started for the corner, but Jarmaine stopped me. She looked nervous but determined. Her eyes darted back and forth.

Finally she said, "Let's sit here."

Jarmaine took the place beside me. She held the basket in her lap like a shield.

The security guard scanned the room. He wasn't much older than some kids I knew at Wellborn High. When his gaze came to rest on us, he slowly walked over.

"You're not allowed here," he told Jarmaine in a rough voice, as if trying to prove he meant it.

She hugged the basket to her chest.

"You hear me?" he said.

"We're not moving," said a voice. I guess it was mine.

"You can stay," he told me. "She has to go."

Jarmaine said something, but I didn't catch it. Neither did the guard.

"What's that?" he asked.

"I said, have you heard of *Boynton versus Virginia*?"

He stared at her blankly.

"It's a Supreme Court case," said Jarmaine. "Last December they ruled that segregation is unconstitutional in bus and train stations where there's interstate commerce."

He didn't answer. She might as well have been speaking Chinese.

"Have you heard of the Freedom Riders?" asked Jarmaine.

"The troublemakers? Yeah, they were here. Bull Connor fixed them." He squinted, eyeing Jarmaine and then me. "Are you with them?"

"Yes," I answered. Well, we were in a way.

"Aren't you kind of young?" asked the guard.

Jarmaine said, "We're students like them."

"Anyway," I said, "my friend and I are sitting together. We're not moving."

There was confusion in his eyes. I saw something else too. It was fear—not of two girls but of the Freedom Riders. The riders had been mocked, beaten, and arrested, but the security guard was afraid of them. They hadn't fought back, and they had earned a kind of power in spite of it—or maybe because of it. The thought made me determined to stay. I didn't want to let them down.

The guard eyed us again, then walked away. For a minute I thought we had won, but he came back with a stern-looking older man. On the pocket of the man's shirt was a badge that said *Station Manager*.

"We don't want trouble," he said.

"Good," I said. "Neither do we."

The station, buzzing just a few minutes before, was quiet. The old man with the sour expression sat a few rows back, watching with a look I'd seen in the crowd at Forsyth's Grocery—mean and stubborn, the face of a person who's been beaten down and wants to fight back. I wondered who had done the beating, and why the man blamed Jarmaine.

There were two dozen passengers in the station, and it seemed that all of them were staring at us. I thought of the mob at Trailways, and suddenly I was afraid.

The manager noticed too. "These people are angry," he said. "They've been through a lot during the past few days. Don't test them."

Jarmaine said, "*They've* been through a lot?"

She glanced around the room and caught the eye of the custodian, who had stopped sweeping and was watching from the corner. He nodded and stood up straight.

Jarmaine turned back to the manager. He met her gaze, then looked away toward the big windows by the door. I wondered if he had expected anything like this when he took the job. For a minute I almost felt sorry for him. He had parents, the same as I did. He had learned some things from them, and he had absorbed other things through his skin and from the air he breathed.

"These people don't want to change," he said.

"What about you?" asked Jarmaine.

He shrugged. "I guess I don't either."

"I do," I said.

"They should whip you," said a voice.

The words came from a sweet-looking lady sitting down the row from us, someone you'd expect to sew a quilt or bring you homemade jam.

A low rumbling started behind us. It spread across the room, the sound of frustration and trouble. A young woman got to her feet and, holding the hand of her little boy, came across the room toward us. She had a pretty face, and her son's cheeks were smudged with jelly. She stopped in front of us.

"You shouldn't sit here," she said. "You never know what people might do."

At first I thought she was being kind, and then I saw her eyes. They were like two black holes, pits you could fall into and never climb out.

Suddenly the man with the sour expression was behind her. Beside me, I heard Jarmaine's rough breathing.

We watched as others got up and came over. It seemed that half the station was there, staring down at us.

I thought of what I had learned in social studies about the Bill of Rights—freedom of speech, freedom of the press, freedom to bear arms. What about freedom to sit? It seemed like such a simple thing.

I reached for Jarmaine's hand. It was damp with sweat. I squeezed, and she squeezed back.

"We're not moving," I said.

CHAPTER
TWENTY-TWO

The woman stepped forward. The people leaned in. We were surrounded by faces and shoulders and fists. Someone grabbed my arm.

Then there was another face. It was dark, ringed below the chin by a thin, white collar. Beneath the collar was a neatly pressed black suit covering a barrel chest and a body the size of a refrigerator. I remembered seeing him in the corner, sitting across a couple of chairs in the colored section.

"What's going on here?" he asked in a deep, smooth voice.

Startled, the station manager stepped back.

"Stay out of this, preacher," he said.

"I can't," said the preacher.

The security guard said, "We got rules."

"I know about rules," said the preacher. "Love God. Love your neighbor."

The guard started to laugh, but it caught in his throat.

The preacher stepped over beside me and put his hand on my shoulder. He faced the crowd and said, "The riders won't stop, you know."

The guard measured us with his gaze. "Yes, they will. We'll make them."

The preacher shook his head. "They'll keep coming. Like these girls, like the others—not just from Nashville but from Chicago and Dallas and Los Angeles. They will come in waves. They will stand strong, and they will not move. You can beat them and curse them and even kill them, and they will keep coming—like the ocean, like the tide, rising to your knees, to your chest, to your chin. America will change. It has to."

He turned to us. "Where are you going?"

"To Montgomery," said Jarmaine. "First Baptist Church, to see the Freedom Riders."

The preacher smiled. "So are we."

I looked over his shoulder and saw that the people from the colored section were standing behind him. They were dressed in Sunday clothes with flowers in their hair and on their lapels. They moved past the white people and filed in wordlessly, taking seats all around us. The crowd hesitated and stepped back.

The station manager started for his desk. "I'm calling the police."

"Sir, it's Sunday morning," said the preacher. "We're going to church."

As the manager picked up the phone, a bus rounded the corner. We heard it pull in behind the station. It was our ride to Montgomery.

We got to our feet, all of us, and moved toward the door. Watching us file out, the station manager put the phone down.

Jarmaine and I showed our tickets to the driver and climbed onto the bus. Without saying a word, we sat in front. Our new friends did too. The preacher patted my shoulder and took the seat behind us.

The white passengers stared and muttered. The bus driver got back on, saw us, and started to say something. He studied my face. I gazed back at him, asking a favor with my eyes. He thought for a minute, then closed the door, got behind the wheel, and guided the bus from the station.

* * *

All of them had baskets. It was a way of traveling I'd

never noticed or thought about—proud, self-contained, able to take care of yourself. Just add wheels. Oh, and a seat, preferably up front. The view is better. The door is closer. The bumps aren't as bad.

Jarmaine shared her food, and our friends shared theirs—cornbread, greens, sweet potato pie. Soon I was so full that if we had gotten a flat tire, I could have taken its place and rolled to Montgomery.

Outside, the scenery had changed. There were low hills and a blue ridge against the horizon. The trees were smaller, and they were evergreens. Every few miles we'd go through a little town—Pelham, Calera, Clanton. We saw lots of churches, some filled with white people, some with black, none with both. For the first time, I thought it was strange.

South of Clanton, the preacher checked the white passengers and leaned forward.

"Those people don't look too happy," he said.

"They'll get used to it," said Jarmaine. "You can get used to almost anything."

The preacher smiled and held out his hand. "I'm Noah. You know, like the ark."

My hand disappeared into his. "I'm Billie. This is Jarmaine. Thanks for helping us."

"I gotta tell you, I was worried," he said. "That security

guard scared me. Young fella, trying to make his mark."

"Not on me," said Jarmaine.

Noah chuckled. "No, indeed."

I asked him, "Where did you come from?"

"God. And Huntsville."

"You're going to Montgomery?" Jarmaine asked. "That's a long trip to church."

He nodded. "Almost two hundred miles."

I said, "We're from Anniston."

"Your town is famous," he said, "for all the wrong reasons."

Jarmaine told him what she had seen at the Anniston bus station, and I described the events in my neighborhood.

"I was in the crowd," I said. "I watched and didn't do anything."

I hated telling him, but in a way it felt good, like a confession.

He eyed me thoughtfully. "Were there grown-ups in the crowd?"

"Yes," I said, "but the only person who helped was a little girl. Her name is Janie."

"Then God bless her," said Noah. "And God bless you."

"For what?"

"Getting on the bus. And standing up to the station manager in Birmingham."

I said, "He wasn't as bad as the others."

"He seemed like a good man," said Noah, "but he was caught in a vise—heart on one side, rules on the other."

It reminded me of my father. He was being squeezed too.

Jarmaine asked Noah, "What have you heard about the meeting tonight?"

"At First Baptist? Dr. King will be there. James Farmer, head of CORE, the Congress of Racial Equality. Fred Shuttlesworth from Birmingham, who works with Dr. King in the Southern Christian Leadership Conference. Ralph Abernathy—it's his church. And of course, the Freedom Riders. Oh, that's right," he said with a twinkle in his eye, "you're with them."

Jarmaine blushed, and I jumped in. "I didn't mean it that way. I just—"

"It's fine," said Noah. "If you ask me, we're all Freedom Riders."

CHAPTER
TWENTY-THREE

Montgomery was a city of hills. Houses, stores, and tall buildings all seemed to perch on the top or bottom of one. The Greyhound station—a surprisingly small one-story building with tan bricks and a thin, gray sign jutting into the air—was halfway down the hill on Court Street. It stood next to a big granite building with fancy pillars, an American flag, and a sign chiseled in stone across the front: Federal Building and United States Courthouse.

Yesterday I'd been at the *Anniston Star* office when Mr. McCall received the call from Montgomery. He had described the riot, and I had tried to imagine it, but only now, arriving on the scene, could I picture what had happened. Jarmaine, who had helped Mr. McCall research the story, filled in the details.

Yesterday the bus from Birmingham, maybe the same one we were on, came down this hill and pulled in behind the station. Hundreds of people surged around it, carrying chains and ropes and bats. They dragged the Freedom Riders off the bus and swarmed over them, beating them without mercy. Some of the riders were knocked unconscious, bleeding, and the crowd kicked them again and again. Photographers like Grant tried to take pictures, but the crowd smashed their cameras and attacked them too.

Jarmaine told me that some of the riders climbed over a wall and tried to take cover in the courthouse. While the flag waved, the mob caught them and pulled them down. The riot lasted for an hour, by which time a thousand people roamed the streets, setting fires and beating anyone with a dark face. Finally, state troopers and mounted sheriff's deputies arrived and dispersed the mob. They arrested just a few people, including a white couple who had been helping the victims. Somehow the Freedom Riders escaped or were taken to the hospital, with the help of some Negro taxi drivers.

Blood and violence filled my mind as we glided down Court Street, its sidewalks empty. I wondered where the rioters were. Maybe they were resting or coming home from church.

The bus reached the station a few minutes after two. The white passengers rose and filed out, while Noah and his friends hung back, letting them go first. It seemed odd, since we had made such a point of sitting in the white seats at the station and on the bus.

Noah must have noticed my confusion, because he smiled and winked. "Got to give them something, right?"

His group closed their baskets and gathered their things, then Jarmaine and I followed them down the steps of the bus and into the loading area behind the station. The driver had opened the luggage compartment and was handing suitcases to the white passengers. When he finished, I saw that the suitcases belonging to Noah and his friends were jammed into a corner of the compartment, separate from the bags of the white passengers.

The driver checked his schedule and headed for the station, leaving the suitcases in the compartment. Noah didn't seem surprised. He nodded to a young man in the group, who began unloading them.

Meanwhile I was eager to see where we were going. I approached a white woman standing nearby.

"Pardon me," I said, "but I'm looking for First Baptist Church."

She led me to the side of the loading area so we could see around the station, then pointed to a beautiful building on the next block with a red, domed roof and a cross on the top.

"That's it," she said. "First Baptist."

I thanked her and returned to the others. Noah and his friends were just getting the last of the bags, and Jarmaine was with them.

Noah turned to me. "Big day."

"Are you going to the church?" Jarmaine asked him.

"Not yet. Some of us have family here. We'll spend the afternoon with them."

He peered toward the station and waved. "There's my sister now. She has a lineup of cars ready for us. Want to come?"

Jarmaine and I exchanged glances.

She said, "I'd like to see the church."

"I found out where it is," I told her.

Turning to Noah, I said, "See you tonight?"

He nodded, smiling, then picked up his suitcase and lumbered off with the others to meet his sister.

Jarmaine and I moved toward the back door of the station and discovered there were two. White passengers filed in through the main door, and Negroes took a side entrance into a dingy, covered area on one side of the building. We might have considered going through the white entrance, but a police officer with a rifle was stationed by the door, probably because of the violence the day before. He glared at us. It made me mad that he had picked us out from among the crowd, but I also felt proud. Maybe Noah was right—we really were Freedom Riders, or at least we looked like them.

Reluctantly we walked through the door marked *Colored Only* and realized we weren't inside the building at all. It really was just part of the alley, where a wooden roof covered a broken-down version of the bus station. The floor was paved with asphalt, and one wall was the outside of the brick building. There was a "lunch counter," which consisted of a little window that opened on the back of the kitchen. The only people there were a haggard-looking woman and her squalling baby. Apparently the other passengers had moved through the area as quickly as they could.

I'd been in three Greyhound stations that day, each more segregated than the last. In Anniston the wall between the races was mostly in people's minds. In Birmingham it was marked off with signs. In Montgomery the wall was made of bricks.

We moved through the station and onto the sidewalk. The sun lit up the street where, just yesterday, the

Freedom Riders had been attacked by a thousand people. I noticed a stain on the sidewalk and wondered if it was blood.

For years I had dreamed of coming here. Sitting on my bed, I had watched the buses rumble by and had imagined myself on them, going to Montgomery. It was the capital of Alabama, where excitement was in the air and important things happened. Now that I was here, something about the place seemed strange and out of kilter, a little bit like my town but bigger and meaner.

Across the street and up the hill was a parking lot, and on the other side, one block over, was the white church with the big, red dome.

"There it is," I told Jarmaine.

"It's beautiful," she said.

Thinking about the meeting and eager to see the place, we hurried off toward First Baptist Church.

CHAPTER TWENTY-FOUR

As we approached the church, Jarmaine stopped.

"Something's wrong," she told me.

"Buses were burned," I said. "People were beaten up and thrown in jail. Of course something's wrong."

"I mean the church."

I studied the building. It looked fine to me. The services were over, but a few people still wandered in and out.

"You don't see it?" asked Jarmaine.

"It's nice."

"The people," she said. "They're white."

What was obvious to Jarmaine had been invisible to me. White was normal. White was fine. You looked right past it and didn't think twice.

In Anniston, I had realized that sometimes Negroes

were invisible to me. Maybe white people were too. Maybe everything was. I'd been drifting through life, sleepwalking, dreaming my silly dreams, thinking I was alive.

It was different for Jarmaine. White was white, black was black, and you'd better know the difference. Life was painful, but you were alert. Colors were bright. Sounds were distinct. Every moment was precious.

I wanted to live that way. The Freedom Riders had jolted me awake. I was rubbing my eyes, trying to take it all in. I wasn't there yet, but I had taken a step or two.

A tall, well-dressed woman walked toward her car, wearing gloves and carrying a big purse. She noticed us and tried to go around, but I stopped her.

"Pardon me," I said, "but is this First Baptist Church?"

"Yes," she said, glancing nervously at Jarmaine.

"Is the meeting tonight?" I asked.

She stared at me blankly.

"You know," said Jarmaine, "the one with Martin Luther King."

The woman drew back, as if the words might soil her gloves. She said, "You must be looking for the other First Baptist Church. It's over on Ripley and Columbus."

Gripping the purse, she hurried off.

In Anniston, there were two schools that called themselves the Panthers. In Montgomery, there were two First Baptist churches. Two worlds, side by side, sharing names, never touching.

Jarmaine watched the woman go, then gazed back at the church. "I thought the building looked awfully nice."

"How do we find the other one?" I asked.

Setting her basket on the sidewalk, Jarmaine dug around inside it and pulled out a map.

"I brought this just in case," she said.

On the front was printed *City of Montgomery*. Jarmaine unfolded the map and spread it on the sidewalk. We found Court Street and the Greyhound station at the lower left. Then, using the index, we searched for Ripley Street. It was eight blocks east, on the right side of the map. Another six blocks north, Columbus Street crossed it. First Baptist Church—the one we wanted— was all the way across the downtown area.

I said, "I guess we should have gone with Noah after all."

Jarmaine shrugged. "We can walk."

"How far is it?" I asked.

She checked the map, measuring the distance with her fingers. "About a mile. You can walk a mile, can't you?"

Jarmaine was smiling, but there was an edge to it. I could almost hear the words in her mind.

Some of us don't have cars or bikes. Some of us use our feet.

"Sure," I said. "Of course."

Jarmaine eyed me, then folded the map, put it away, and picked up the basket.

"Follow me," she said.

* * *

From the bus, the hills had been pretty. On foot they didn't seem that way.

It was fine at first. From the domed church we went downhill on Perry Street. Since it was Sunday, the stores and office buildings were closed. There were only a few people around, most of them Negroes who, like us, were walking.

It was turning out to be a hot day. I wished I'd brought a hat to block the sun, and I wasn't thrilled with the shoes I had chosen. I had pictured myself in church and had put on a pair of white sandals to go with my dress, never stopping to think that the straps might bind and the soles were as thin as paper. After a few blocks I was already limping. When Jarmaine noticed, she just shook her head.

At the bottom of the hill we looked off to our right and saw the Alabama State Capitol, high on a hill. I'd seen pictures of it in schoolbooks but never in person. It had columns across the front and a big dome on top.

The building had always seemed perfect to me, but now, thinking about the Freedom Riders, I wasn't so sure.

Then we started uphill. It was like walking from Forsyth's Grocery to my house, times ten. I felt every pebble and bump. My pretty summer dress hung on me like a tent, and it was soaked under the arms.

We passed a store with a sign on top shaped like a boot, with words on it: *Old Shoes Made New*. I could have used some help, but of course the store was closed. Jarmaine, up ahead, just kept walking. She had on a comfortable pair of shoes, like the ones Lavender wore at our house. Jarmaine had been carrying the basket for the whole trip, and suddenly that didn't seem right.

"Can I carry the basket?" I asked.

She took one look at me and laughed. That didn't sit too well, so I stepped forward and grabbed it.

"Hey," she said.

"Get used to it. We're on the same team, you know."

She laughed again, but this time it didn't sound so bad.

We went up a hill and down another. When we got to Columbus Street, we turned right. We spotted a bench at the bus stop and plopped down for a rest and a snack. After a few minutes we set out again.

Guess what: a hill. Columbus Street was a long, steady slope, with a redbrick building like a beacon at the top. I carried the basket and transferred it from hand to hand, sweating like a pig in a dress. I lowered my head and put one foot in front of the other.

Finally, I looked up again. We were standing at the top of the hill. The redbrick building loomed overhead. On the side of the building, in a glass-covered case, was a sign: *First Baptist Church*.

I heard organ music.

CHAPTER
TWENTY-FIVE

The song was "Amazing Grace," and the notes spilled out like water. Every so often they would pause, swirl, and tumble on. They formed a river and then a waterfall, pouring over the edge and crashing below.

I stepped back and studied the building. It was like a castle with a cross on top. The base was built of smooth, brown stones, and the red bricks, actually more of a rust color, had been stacked on top of those. On the Columbus side was a big stained-glass window with an arch on top. The church faced Ripley Street, and on the front were two towers, one taller than the other. The big tower, at the corner, had four points at the top, and just below those, on each side, were two open spaces looking out over the street like eyes. Between the two towers, at street level, were concrete steps leading up to an imposing front door. We climbed them and went inside.

The lobby—church people called it the narthex—was painted bright white, and the sun shone through the windows to make it glow. Straight ahead, a set of doors had been thrown open and music poured out. It wasn't a hymn this time but scales, starting slowly and picking up speed. We approached cautiously and peered through the doorway.

It was a cavernous room with row after row of curved wooden pews, red carpet leading to the front, and, at the side, the stained-glass window we'd seen from the street, blue and green and purple, lit up like a torch. The ceiling arched high overhead. There was a balcony at the back. In front was a big wooden pulpit, with banks of golden organ pipes covering the wall behind it.

"Yoo-hoo!"

The music had stopped. I looked around to see who was calling. There was movement off to one side of the pulpit, then a hand sticking up from behind the organ console, waving. Jarmaine and I made our way hesitantly to the front. As we approached, I realized the wooden console was huge, the size of a boat.

I figured the organist must be huge too, like the Wizard of Oz that Dorothy and her friends had imagined. But, like the real Oz, the person behind the console turned out to be small and stoop shouldered. Seated on a gleaming wooden bench, with keyboards in front of her and pedals below, was a little brown lady. She wore a flowered dress, her hair was pulled into a bun, and she was smiling.

"Beautiful, isn't it?" she said.

My gaze swept across the sanctuary. "This is yours?"

"Not the church," she said. "The music."

Jarmaine said, "We heard 'Amazing Grace.'"

The woman nodded. "I always play that first. Gets the juices flowing. Then I do scales to warm up my fingers."

"They seem pretty warm already," I said.

She chuckled. "My husband used to say that. Played the trumpet. My but he could blow that horn. He passed ten years ago."

"I'm sorry," said Jarmaine.

"He's with the Lord. They're jammin' right now. Sometimes late at night, I hear them."

I asked, "Is the meeting here? You know, for the Freedom Riders."

"Yes, indeed. Eight o'clock tonight. You coming?"

"We're here," said Jarmaine.

"You're early."

"So are you," I told her.

She studied me, friendly but curious. "What's your name?"

"Billie. This is Jarmaine."

"I'm Gussie Mae Hall. You can call me Gus. Everyone does."

She held out her hand, and both of us shook it. Her fingers really were warm.

"Why are you so early?" I asked.

She noodled a few notes on the keyboard, and the sanctuary came alive.

"Well, it's this way," said Gus. "Husband is gone, son off at school. What else am I going to do?"

"Are you playing for the meeting?" asked Jarmaine.

"Sweetheart, I play for everything. Weddings, funerals, services—me and the Lord, we always show up."

I had to smile. Gus talked about the Lord like he was somebody she saw every day, and maybe she did.

Since Gus had shared, I figured we could too.

"We came to see the Freedom Riders," I told her.

"And Dr. King," added Jarmaine. She described our trip from Anniston. I told what had happened to us on the bus and in the station.

Gus stared. "You integrated the Birmingham

Greyhound station? Two teenage girls?" She snorted. "You're either foolish or brave."

"We had help," I said, thinking of Noah and his friends.

Jarmaine yawned. I wondered how early she had gotten up that morning to catch the bus. Gus noticed too.

"There's time before the meeting," she said. "You want a place to lie down?"

Jarmaine glanced at me, and I gave a little nod. Suddenly I was tired too.

"Yes, ma'am," Jarmaine told her. "Thank you."

"I know just the place," said Gus. "It's quiet, and no one will bother you."

"Is there a bathroom?" I asked. "That's one thing we didn't integrate."

Gus smiled. She slid out from behind the organ and showed us the restrooms. Afterward, she took us to a tall staircase off to one side of the narthex. Light streamed down the stairs from windows at the top. As we followed Gus up, I looked at the wooden steps, worn smooth and polished, and thought of all the people who had climbed them.

Gus must have heard me thinking. "This building was finished in 1915," she said, "but the first one was built in 1867, two years after the Civil War. Slaves used to worship at First Baptist on Perry Street, where they had to stay in the balcony. When emancipation came, a bunch of them rose up one Sunday, marched across town, and declared they were starting their own church right here."

So, the two First Baptists used to be one church. They had touched after all.

At the top of the staircase was a door into the balcony, with more pews looking down on the organ pipes and pulpit.

"This is nice," I said, eyeing the pews and thinking I'd like to lie down on one.

"Yes, it is," said Gus, "but it's not where we're going."

She started up a second flight of stairs. They took us to an attic with rough wooden floors and brick walls, where boxes and equipment were stacked. I looked for a place to lie down. I didn't say anything, but the balcony seemed nicer.

The ceiling had open beams, and a ladder came down from between two of them. To my surprise, Gus knotted the hem of her dress and mounted the first step.

"Where are you going?" asked Jarmaine.

Gus said, "You'll see."

She nearly bumped her head at the top, then reached up and pushed on the ceiling. I was amazed to see a rectangle open up and swing back. It was a trapdoor. Apparently the attic had an attic. Sunshine poured through. Gus's head disappeared, then her shoulders, and finally her legs and feet. Jarmaine and I looked at each other.

I shrugged. "Here goes."

Climbing the ladder, I stuck my head through the opening and into the light.

CHAPTER
TWENTY-SIX

It might have been heaven.

We were in a room that was more than a room. Brick walls opened wide all around, two windows on each. I realized we were in the big tower. If the windows were eyes, as they had seemed from the street below, then we were behind them, gazing out.

I scrambled up into the room, then turned and helped Jarmaine climb through the opening with her basket. We stood up and looked around.

"My daddy brought me up here when I was a little girl," said Gus. "Years later I brought my son. I'll bring my grandchildren too, Lord willing."

Gus stepped aside, and we saw what was behind her. In the middle of the space was a big metal wheel like a gear, braced by a network of two-by-fours, all of it painted the same rust color as the bricks. A railing wrapped around it, and above, hanging from the ceiling, was a heavy iron brace shaped like shoulders. Below it, where the heart would be, hung a giant bell. It was gray with white splotches, like an ancient rock you'd find in a field. On the bell, in raised letters, was a list of names, apparently deacons in the church. And there was a message.

PEACE ON EARTH, GOOD WILL TO MEN
REV. A. JACKSON STOKES
EST. 1866

"I thought the church was built in 1867," said Jarmaine.

Gus smiled. "It was. Can you figure out why the bell shows a different year?"

I studied the words, as if the answer might be written in code. Then it hit me. "The building was done in 1867, but the church started before that."

"You've got it. The congregation formed in 1866 and raised the first building a year later. But it was made of wood, and in 1910 it burned down. So they rebuilt it, using bricks. In fact, they called it the Brick-a-Day Church, because church members brought a brick a day to help with the building. When it was finished, they had this bell made for the tower. You might say the church was built to hold it."

Jarmaine murmured.

"What was that?" I asked her.

"Something my mother used to tell me. 'First you dream it; then you build it.'"

I thought of Daddy sitting on my bed at night, giving me words to think about. Lavender must have done the same with Jarmaine.

Beneath the bell was a square opening going all the way down to the first floor. Two thick ropes hung from the bell, brushing the railing three stories below.

"Would you like to hear it?" asked Gus.

The idea startled me. "The bell? Is that allowed?"

"We ring it Sunday morning and on special occasions. I'd say this is a special occasion, wouldn't you?"

I nodded eagerly.

"Why are there two ropes?" asked Jarmaine.

Gus reached over the railing and touched one of them. "When you pull the first rope, there's a single toll. That's for funerals, sending a soul to heaven. The second one's for Sunday morning. It rings the bell over and over again—you know, like a celebration."

Gus handed the second rope to Jarmaine. "Go ahead. Pull."

Jarmaine's eyes opened wide. The rope lay in her palms like a prize. The daughter of a daughter of a daughter of slaves, she gripped the rope and gazed at the bell. She pulled, hard, as if trying to break their chains.

The tower erupted. If the organ music had been a river, this was the ocean, wide and deep. It started as a low moan, then shook the tower like an earthquake. I could feel myself vibrate. The sound was inside my chest. The bell was ringing me.

Watching it, I was surprised. "I thought the clapper would swing, but it doesn't move."

Gus smiled. "The clapper is still, and the bell swings around it."

I liked that. Maybe I could ring too, if I just stood still enough. Then the people and the world and the sky and stars could swing around me.

When the ringing died out, Jarmaine handed the rope back to Gus. I walked to one of the windows, and Jarmaine followed. The opening, one of eight around the room, started at our shoes and ended a foot over our heads, with an arch on top. I stretched out my arms and barely touched the sides. Up close, I realized the opening was actually covered with wire mesh so no one would fall.

We were looking down on Ripley Street, at the front of the church. Diagonally across the intersection of Ripley and Columbus was a grassy, parklike area with graves.

"That's old Oakwood Cemetery," said Gus, who had come up behind us. "It started out in the early 1800s as Scott's Free Burying Ground, because it was free to everyone, even Negroes, and in Montgomery that was unusual. Behind the original section there's a newer part called the annex, which includes graves for members of England's Royal Air Force, who trained here during World War II, and the country music singer Hank Williams."

I said, "Hank Williams? He's one of my daddy's favorites. He sang 'I'm So Lonesome I Could Cry.'"

Gus looked out over the rows of graves. "I guess some of the slaves would have agreed with that."

Directly across Ripley Street was another grassy area with trees and benches.

"That's our park," said Gus.

"The church owns it?" I asked.

She and Jarmaine exchanged looks.

Gus said, "Not the church—the people. It's the only park in Montgomery where Negroes are allowed."

I thought of the parks we had ridden by in the bus and had walked by on our way across town. Apparently they were for whites only.

"Really?" I said.

"You're learning a lot on this trip," said Jarmaine.

I pointed to the park. "Then what are those white people doing?"

A group of about twenty men milled around, talking and smoking. A line of cars and pickup trucks was parked nearby.

Gus's eyes narrowed, and she grew thoughtful.

"I don't know," she said.

"It can't be good," said Jarmaine.

CHAPTER
TWENTY-SEVEN

Gus found blankets for us, then left us there to nap. I stretched out and tried to sleep but couldn't. When I closed my eyes, I could still see the bell and hear it ringing.

After a few minutes, I opened my eyes. Jarmaine had been lying next to me, but she had gotten up and was sitting by the window, hugging her knees to her chest. Her face reflected the afternoon sun. I'd seen before that she was proud and determined. Now I saw that she was pretty. The sun made her skin the color of coffee mixed with cream. She had long lashes and deep brown eyes.

"What do you see?" I asked.

"I was thinking. I miss my mother. I feel bad about sneaking off. I didn't want her to worry, but now she will."

I pictured Lavender and tried to imagine what she was doing. It occurred to me that Lavender often looked worried, but I hadn't noticed. There were lots of things about her that I hadn't noticed or had taken for granted—her soft touch, her gentle voice, the way she brushed my hair.

"When I was little," said Jarmaine, "sometimes I had trouble sleeping. She would sit on the bed and sing a lullaby—'Hush, Little Baby.' It made me feel safe. Then I could fall asleep. But she would still be worried. You raise up your children and protect them, then you have to let them go. They make mistakes and get hurt and run off without telling you."

"We're doing what's right," I said.

"It's right for us. Hard for our parents."

"Our mothers still love us. They have to."

Jarmaine shook her head. "They don't have to do anything."

"Yes, they do," I said. "They have to love us. It sounds selfish, but it's true."

Jarmaine grunted. I could tell she was thinking about it.

"Fathers too," I said.

She looked up at me, and I remembered she had never met her father.

"Oh, I'm sorry."

"What's it like?" asked Jarmaine.

"Having a father?"

It was something else I hadn't thought of. It just was.

"I like it, I guess. He's not like Mama. He's loud. He tells stories. We play football. People like him and want to be around him. I don't know—he's just Daddy."

I thought of the disagreements he sometimes had with Lavender. "What does your mom say about him?" I asked.

"You want a nice story or the truth?"

I swallowed hard. "The truth."

"Promise you won't tell anyone?"

"Yes."

"She doesn't like him," said Jarmaine.

She watched me for a reaction. I tried not to show it, but it hurt.

"She doesn't like many white people," Jarmaine added quickly.

"I thought she was, you know, part of our family," I said.

"My mother has a family," said Jarmaine. "There are two people in it."

Maybe Jarmaine was trying to make me feel bad. She had succeeded.

"If we're not her family, what are we?" I asked.

Jarmaine studied my face. "You ever see a water moccasin?"

"The snake?"

She nodded. "They live in marshes and streams. They're poison. Step on them, and you die."

"You think we're like that?" I asked.

"White people are dangerous. That's what my mother told me."

Lavender swept our floor and set our table and made apple cobbler, all the while believing we were dangerous. The thought was alien, like we had landed on the planet Mars.

Jarmaine gazed out the window and shook her head. "You and I are different. I told you that before."

"It doesn't have to be that way," I said.

"Oh really?"

"Look at us. We're doing this together, right?"

"You think that makes us alike?"

"Maybe we want the same things," I said.

"Look, Billie, you mean well, but let's face it. White people want to keep us down. It's always been that way."

"Not all of them," I said. "What about Mr. McCall? What about Grant?"

She shrugged. "They're not like the others."

"So, there's hope for me?"

Jarmaine chuckled. "You don't give up, do you?"

"No, I don't. And you know who taught me that? My father, the man Lavender doesn't like. The man who watched the bus burn. What do you think of that?"

She got to her feet and stretched. "I think I'm tired."

"Me too. Come lie down. There's still time to sleep."

Jarmaine settled onto the floor next to me. I pulled the blanket over her, and she curled up like I'd seen Royal do. She closed her eyes, and I began to sing.

"Hush, little baby, don't say a word. Papa's gonna buy you a mockingbird…"

Lavender had sung it to me too, years ago when she had put me down for a nap. I wondered why she sang a lullaby about a father. I wondered what it would be like to have a baby and see her grow up. I remembered the disease Lavender had told me about, the one that made us dangerous, the one that rocked the bus and set it on fire, the one that could hurt people just by watching. I wondered if I still had it and if I would pass it on.

CHAPTER
TWENTY-EIGHT

I dreamed I was walking with Daddy. He held my hand and spoke to me. I couldn't understand his words, but the sound of his voice made me feel good. A pickup truck was parked ahead of us. We got in, and a crowd formed. They rocked the truck and beat on it with their fists. A man picked up a rock and smashed the window. In the distance, over the crowd, I heard a bell.

When I woke up, the bell hung above me. The gray surface was tinged with orange. I checked my watch and saw that it was six o'clock. We had been sleeping for nearly two hours. I climbed to my feet and hurried to a window, where the orange light streamed in. To the west, the sun was dipping toward the hills. As I watched, it went behind a cloud, and bright rays spread across the sky. Suddenly I thought of Grant and wished he were there to see it.

I moved away from the window and shook Jarmaine's shoulder. "Jarmaine, get up."

She looked at me, confused, then saw the brick walls and remembered where she was. Together we moved to the east windows, looked out over Ripley Street, and realized that things had changed. People were flooding into the church from all directions, on foot and by car. There were hundreds of them, maybe more. The men wore coats and ties, the women hats and colorful dresses. The children, excited, skipped along behind, showing their Sunday best.

Across the street, the small group of white men had grown too. Now it was a big crowd, filling the park and spilling out into the streets. Some of the men gripped pipes and chains as they watched the worshipers. A few tried to block their path, but the worshipers pushed on through.

"I don't like the looks of that," said Jarmaine.

Sounds billowed up from below. There were happy voices, snatches of conversation, a bottle breaking. Somewhere in the distance, a dog barked.

I noticed a station wagon inching up Ripley, through the crowd and toward the church. Other cars had parked, but this driver seemed determined to reach the front door, and I wondered why.

Slowly, agonizingly, the car drew closer. Finally, at a curb by the corner, it stopped and two Negroes got out. The driver was a teenager. The passenger, wearing a beautiful black suit and a hat that was tipped to hide his face, was a man with broad shoulders and a dignified way of carrying himself.

"Oh my God," said Jarmaine.

"What?"

"That's Dr. King," she said.

"Martin Luther King?"

"They said he was flying in from Atlanta. He must have come from the airport."

Jarmaine started to call out but caught herself, pressing her hand over her mouth as if to bottle up a dangerous secret. On the street below, the driver got a suitcase from the back of the car and pushed his way through the crowd, with Dr. King following behind, his face still hidden. Even so, there was something about him that made you sit up and take notice.

The worshipers were the first to recognize him. Some of them kept quiet, but others, thrilled, reached out to touch him. A child shouted his name. The men in the park heard it. You could see the word passing like a flame. It spread, and they surged toward him.

Next to me, Jarmaine shouted, "Watch out!"

Dr. King checked behind him. The driver yelled something to the worshipers. As if they had planned it, the people edged toward Dr. King, forming a barrier around him.

"There he is!" shouted the men. "Get him!"

Fists swung. A pipe caught the afternoon sun. People stumbled, but the group kept moving, and so did Dr. King. Rocks flew. Dr. King ducked. Someone held up a Bible.

Finally the group arrived at the front door, directly below us. Dr. King took off his hat and gazed up at the church. He saw us in the tower and smiled.

I waved. "Hello!"

"Be careful," called Jarmaine.

Brown hands reached out. Gently but firmly, they pulled Dr. King through the door. The white men backed off, grumbling. The worshipers buzzed with excitement. Over it all, like the soundtrack of a movie, we heard organ music—"Babylon's Falling," "I'll Fly Away," and other hymns I didn't recognize.

Gus was at her post, and I wanted to join her.

CHAPTER TWENTY-NINE

We hurried down the ladder, through the attic, past the balcony, and into the narthex. It was crammed with people moving slowly but steadily into the sanctuary, where they were seated by ushers who had carnations in their lapels.

Jarmaine asked one of the ushers, "Where's Dr. King?"

"Downstairs. He'll be back when the meeting starts."

We slipped into the sanctuary and made our way across the rear, then along the wall beneath the big stained-glass window. I don't know why, but suddenly I was aware that the room was filled with Negroes. They had always been there at the edges of my town and my life, off to the side, but now I was the one at the edge, an outsider, someone who looked different and didn't fit in. This was their place. Other white faces dotted the crowd, but there were just a few of us.

Jarmaine eyed me. "How does it feel? You know, being a minority."

"Do they want me here?" I asked.

"Some do, some don't. A lot of them don't even see you. You're invisible. You don't exist."

There was pain in her eyes.

"Like you?" I asked.

"Sometimes."

"It feels strange," I said. "It makes me nervous."

"Scared?" said Jarmaine.

"Maybe a little bit."

She searched my face. "Why did you come?"

I shrugged. "I thought you could use a friend."

"Are we friends?"

"We could be," I said.

"Black and white?"

I had to smile. Sometimes on summer afternoons, Mama made hot fudge sundaes. She called them black and whites.

"Sure," I said. "I'm the ice cream. You're the fudge."

"I don't understand."

I told her about the sundaes. "Maybe I'll make one for you sometime."

"I'd like that," she said.

"Billie!" called a voice.

Apparently someone in the crowd did know me. Surprised, I looked around. In the sea of dark faces I spotted Noah, gigantic, his hand raised in greeting and his friends spread out around him. Noah grinned, and I waved back.

In front, directly ahead of us, was the organ console where Gus, tiny but fierce, was in her glory. Instead of a single keyboard, the organ had three—two stacked like ledges in front of her, and a giant one below for her feet. When she played, her whole body was involved, moving, swiveling, dancing. I wondered how organists could ever go back to playing the piano.

Instead of waiting for the preachers, the people had started without them. They stood and sang, waving their arms in the air. Every few seconds someone would call out: "That's right!" "Lord Jesus!" "Yes, indeed!" I had heard about churches like this but had never been inside one. The closest I'd come had been late at night, listening to the radio, tuning in stations from Memphis and Atlanta, when the music had poured out like syrup.

There were three arches across the front of the sanctuary, echoing the arch of the stained-glass window. Behind the pulpit, the center arch was the biggest, with steps leading to an altar that was lined with beautiful dark wood and crimson carpet. Beyond the altar, towering over the room, was the bank of organ pipes, and beneath that were chairs like thrones for the pastor and other church officials.

The smaller arches on either side had a low, wood-paneled railing across the front, and behind the railing was the choir loft. Some choir members were already there—standing, singing, clapping, their blue robes flowing as they moved. Beside them were some other people who weren't wearing robes.

Jarmaine and I made our way to the front. I noticed a place behind the organ bench where we could sit and lean against the wall, just below the choir loft. That's when I noticed how hot it was. The day had been warm, and the heat had settled in the sanctuary. The crowd, stuffed into the room like sardines, must have numbered well over a thousand. I saw the flash of paper fans as people tried to stay cool, but it wasn't working.

Gus looked back and winked at us. She played the final notes of "A City Called Heaven." Then, instead of stopping, she played chords with her left hand while thumbing through the hymnal with her right.

The congregation might have paused, but Gus didn't. She found a hymn she liked and flattened the page with her hand. Before she played again, she rocked back on the bench in our direction. She nodded toward the choir members right above us.

"That's them, you know."

"Who?" I asked.

"Who else?" she said. "The Freedom Riders."

I jumped to my feet and whirled around. The choir loft was above us, at shoulder height, so that even when standing, I had to crane my neck to see over the railing. There were flashes of color when the choir moved. Then I took a step back, and the people beside them came into view, wearing suits and dresses but no robes.

The Freedom Riders loomed over us, like actors in a movie when you sit in the front row. I looked more closely and saw that they didn't seem like movie stars at all but regular people—smiling, some bruised and swollen, a few I dimly recognized from news photos.

Gus leaned back on the bench and explained. "We wanted people to notice them, so we put them in the loft. God's choir, I call them."

There must have been twenty of them. After the riot in downtown Montgomery, a second group from Nashville had arrived to show support for the first group of ten.

Beside me, Jarmaine scanned their faces and recited

the names. "John Lewis. Lucretia Collins. Catherine Burks. Bernard Lafayette. Salynn McCollum. I guess Jim Zwerg and William Barbee are in the hospital. There's James Lawson—he's the one who trained them in nonviolence."

Jarmaine gasped, and her hand flew to her mouth.

"What?" I said.

"Next to James Lawson. That's Diane Nash. She's here!"

Watching Jarmaine, I thought it must be exciting and a little unsettling to see your hopes and dreams standing in front of you. They live in a corner of your mind, safe and secure, and suddenly there they are in person, real but unpredictable.

As we watched, a man came up and whispered something to Diane Nash. She nodded grimly, excused herself, and followed him out of the choir loft.

Gus played hymn after hymn, and the people sang along. I felt like I was floating in a sea of music, eyes closed, face toward heaven. It felt different from my church. There, the people sat in their own little corner, tuning in and out of the service. Here, you couldn't tune out if you wanted to. The music grabbed you and wouldn't let go.

At eight o'clock, a heavyset man with glasses and a receding hairline stepped to the pulpit.

"Praise God, we made it!"

The crowd roared. I wondered how there could be so much love inside the building and so much hate outside.

The man smiled and said, "I'm Reverend Solomon Seay, pastor of Mount Zion AME over here on Holt Street. Tonight I have the best job in town. I get to introduce the saints of our movement—Dr. King, Ralph Abernathy, Fred Shuttlesworth, James Farmer of CORE, and of course the Freedom Riders."

The cheer was deafening. Jarmaine and I stood up again to see them. Reverend Seay named the Freedom Riders one by one without notes, and Jarmaine explained that Seay knew them because they had spent the night at his house. Then he introduced Dr. King and the other leaders. As a group the leaders walked over—right above us, close enough to touch—and hugged the Freedom Riders, with the same kind of awe on their faces that I'd seen on Jarmaine's.

I realized there might be only a few white people in the room, but some of those were Freedom Riders. After all, the riders weren't just Negroes. They were black and white, a mix. Wasn't that the point? Besides sitting in the front of the bus, they also had sat together, an integrated group in a segregated world.

By getting on the bus with their Negro friends, the white riders had earned their way into First Baptist Church. There were just a few of them, but they belonged here. Maybe I did too. I had walked with Jarmaine into the Greyhound station. I had climbed onto the bus with her. I had faced an angry crowd in Birmingham, and I hadn't backed down. After a lifetime of watching, I had decided to ride. Wasn't that worth something?

As the leaders filed back toward the pulpit, an explosion ripped through the night.

CHAPTER
THIRTY

Gus flew off the bench, wrapped an arm around each of us, and pushed us to the floor. Stunned, we huddled like that for a few moments. When I got the nerve to look up, I saw flames through one of the windows.

The mob was close now, rumbling dangerously. The sound seemed familiar, and I remembered where I had heard it. It was in Anniston, when the crowd had attacked the bus.

In the church there were screams and yells. Children cried. Some people crouched under the pews. Others pushed and shoved, trying to get out but with nowhere to go. I tried to imagine what would happen if the church caught fire, and I realized how frightened the riders must have been that day in Anniston—trapped, unable to escape, surrounded by flames.

Through the confusion, Reverend Seay hurried to the pulpit and leaned toward the microphone. "Folks, we just got word that it wasn't a bomb. Somebody tipped a car over, and the gas tank blew up. That's all it was."

He glanced toward Gus. "Now, how about some music?"

Gus straightened up, then struggled to her feet and climbed back onto the bench. Her fingers found the keys, and she leaned into a hymn that Lavender had sung around our house, "Love Lifted Me."

Reverend Seay boomed, "Come on, now! I want you to lift your voices and mean every word of it."

A few people sang. More joined in. Little by little, the panic ebbed as people heard the familiar words.

But the flames didn't stop, and neither did the mob. At the pulpit, the leaders huddled. A group of them, including Dr. King, headed toward the narthex.

"Where are they going?" asked Jarmaine.

"Let's find out," I said.

We scrambled up the aisle. Reverend Abernathy, a rugged-looking man with broad shoulders and a neat mustache, led the way through his church, with Dr. King at his shoulder and James Farmer behind. Reaching the narthex, they turned right and went down a staircase toward the basement, talking earnestly. We followed at a distance, hoping no one would see us.

The staircase had two flights, and on the landing between them was a little window looking out onto Ripley Street, just above the sidewalk. We paused there and gazed outside.

It was a street-level view of hell.

People crowded up against the church, yelling, drinking, screaming to the skies. Some had wrapped chains around their fists. Others gripped pipes and bats. Through a forest of knees, I saw a man crouch down and pour gasoline into a bottle, stuff one end of a rag into it, and light the other end. Grinning, he stood up and threw the bottle toward the church. There was a crash and the flash of another fire. Beyond the flames was a sea of angry faces.

I said, "What are we going to do?"

"Follow Dr. King," said Jarmaine.

At the bottom of the staircase, off to our left, church members scurried around the kitchen, wearing aprons and hairnets. A few of them pulled food from a massive refrigerator, while others stirred giant pots on the stove using big wooden spoons, trying to pretend this was just another church social.

Straight ahead, opposite the staircase, was a small

room with a sign above it: *Office*. The leaders filed inside. I expected them to shut the door, but between the boiling pots and the heat outside, the basement was sweltering, so they left it open. Reverend Abernathy offered his desk to Dr. King, who sat down and hung his coat on the back of the chair. Abernathy and Farmer leaned down, and the three of them talked in low voices.

Jarmaine asked, "What are they saying?"

"Let's get closer," I said.

As we stepped off the staircase, a young man appeared next to us. Just a few years older than we were, he looked familiar, but I couldn't remember from where.

"What are you doing here?" he asked.

Jarmaine spoke for us. I was happy to let her. "Looking around. It's a beautiful church."

"It's nicer upstairs," he said. "Why don't you go up there?"

He looked toward the office, where Dr. King was on the phone, and I remembered where I had seen him.

"You drove Dr. King," I said. "We saw you in front of the church."

He eyed me uneasily, then asked Jarmaine, "Who is she?"

"She's my friend," said Jarmaine. "We came to see Dr. King. What's he like?"

"He's a great man. He even asked me about my school."

Jarmaine grinned. "What did you tell him?"

The young man smiled sheepishly. "School's hard. He said to keep trying. Keep the faith."

I glanced around and noticed a couple of chairs against the wall just outside the office door, where people could sit and wait to meet with the pastor.

I said, "We're kind of tired. You think we could sit in those chairs?"

He looked at the office, then back at Jarmaine.

She said, "We've come a long way."

The young man ducked his head and nodded. "I guess so. Sure, go ahead."

"Thank you," she said.

He stood there awkwardly for a moment. There was a crash somewhere outside, and he blinked. "I'd better go."

He hurried upstairs. I walked over to the chairs and sat in one of them. Jarmaine followed and settled in beside me.

I said, "He liked you."

"Shhh."

We heard snatches of conversation coming from the office. "...dangerous...troops...the governor..." There was the click of a telephone receiver and the whir of a dial. A few moments later, Dr. King said in that unmistakable voice of his, "Yes? Mr. Attorney General? Sir, the situation here is desperate. You've got to do something."

Jarmaine's eyes opened wide and she whispered, "He's talking to President Kennedy's brother, Robert Kennedy."

It was hard to imagine. There we were, in the basement of an Alabama church, hearing Martin Luther King talk to the White House on the same phone that church members used when they ordered beans and ham.

Dr. King described the scene outside the church, then said, "No, sir. There's no police, no highway patrol. We're surrounded. Federal marshals? Well, if they don't get here immediately, we're going to have a bloody confrontation."

In the kitchen, pots and pans clattered, drowning out the voices. When the noise stopped, Dr. King was saying, "A cooling-off period? I'll ask them. But first we need those federal marshals."

James Farmer went shooting out the door and up the stairs, a look of alarm on his face. Inside the office, Dr. King finished the call. By the time he hung up, Farmer was back, and someone was with him.

It was Diane Nash.

Up close she was beautiful, with high cheekbones, flowing hair, and skin the color of caramel. Jarmaine stared. I guess she couldn't help it. I elbowed her, afraid someone would tell us to leave, but the two of them hurried on by.

Inside the office, Dr. King told them, "The Attorney General asked if we could end the Freedom Rides. He suggested a cooling-off period."

Farmer answered, "If we do, we'll just get words and promises."

"I'm not so sure," said Dr. King. "We've made our point. The nation's watching. Now they know."

"Sir," said Diane Nash in a sweet, steely voice, "with all due respect, that's wrong."

Beside me, Jarmaine gasped. I wondered how often people spoke like that to Dr. King.

"Just listen," said Nash.

Up the stairs, beyond the windows, I could hear the mob coiling, ready to strike. Chains rattled. Glass shattered. Someone pounded on the church doors.

Nash said, "If we stop now, we'll be giving in to that. The Freedom Rides have to continue."

Dr. King told her, "Your people may die."

"Then others will follow."

"Do they know what they're doing?" asked Abernathy.

"Sir," said Diane Nash, "you should know that before we left, all of us drew up our wills. We know that we might be killed, but we can't let violence overcome nonviolence."

"She's right," Farmer declared. "We've been cooling off for three hundred and fifty years. If we cool off any more, we'll be in the deep freeze. The Freedom Rides will go on."

I glanced at Jarmaine. She looked scared but hopeful.

Abernathy said, "There are fifteen hundred people upstairs. I think they'll want to know."

"Then let's go," said Dr. King.

CHAPTER THIRTY-ONE

Dr. King came out of the office and put on his coat. Behind him were Abernathy and Farmer. Diane Nash came last. She noticed us and smiled, lighting up the room.

We followed them at a safe distance and slipped back into the sanctuary. The church meeting had been going on while we were in the basement. Some of the Freedom Riders were by the pulpit, and Gus was at the organ, rocking through another hymn.

I wished Grant was there to take pictures and sing along. I remembered how he had looked up at the bus as Jarmaine and I rode by. After what he had seen and photographed that day at Forsyth's, he deserved to be with us. I could have stopped on the way to the bus station and picked him up. Sometimes I got mad at him for doing things and not including me, and now I had done the same to him. Grant was my friend. He might be more than that, but it would never happen unless I gave him a chance.

Dr. King went to the front, and Gus ended the music. The people settled down. Fans swished back and forth, and handkerchiefs wiped foreheads, but the crowd was quiet.

Dr. King leaned over the microphone and said, "The first thing to know is that we're going to be calm, and we're going to continue to stand up for what we know is right. We are not giving in. The Freedom Rides will go on."

Someone shouted, "Amen!" Others joined in, and Dr. King held up his hand for silence.

"The second thing to know is that I just got off the phone with Robert Kennedy. He's sending in federal marshals. They're going to get us out of here."

A cheer went up. I couldn't help but notice there was grumbling too. Maybe some of the people didn't want to be rescued. They would stand with Dr. King, flames or no flames.

There were more speeches and more hymns. I turned to Jarmaine. "I'd sure like to see those federal marshals."

She gazed back thoughtfully. "We can, you know."

Grabbing my hand, she led me out of the sanctuary, up the stairs, and into the church attic. We could hear distant voices below, but the attic was quiet. We made our way up the ladder, pushed open the door, and climbed through.

Did you ever wonder what heaven is like at night? I had always pictured it during the day, with bright blue skies and puffy, white clouds. But until I stepped into that tower again, I had never imagined it at night.

There's darkness. There's a breeze that ruffles your hair. There are windows all around. There's a sky filled with stars. There are sturdy brick walls. In the center, there's a bell.

It's an ancient bell, and on it are the names of the saints. They have worked and planned and persevered. They have been cursed and beaten, driven from their homes and shipped to a cruel land. Their children have been taken away and their families torn apart. They have bent under blows, but they have gotten up again. They have worshiped. They have sung. And on special days, when the world seems about to burst, the bell rings, the sun rises, and the saints dance with joy.

The thoughts filled my mind, as if poured from a pitcher. I wondered who they came from—Dr. King,

Jarmaine, the people crowded together downstairs. Maybe thoughts came from places. In my neighborhood, we thought about ourselves and the way we had always done things. Tradition, we called it. On Jarmaine's block, there was fear. If you saw a white person, you wondered what was wrong. In this church, around this bell, there was love, mixed with hope and determination and fierce pride. It filled the place, and it filled me. It felt like heaven.

There's something else about heaven. If you look down, you can see hell. We had gotten the street view from the basement, and now we saw it from above. Jarmaine and I stood at a window, watching.

The crowd had turned into a mob, surrounding the church and throwing itself against the doors. Angry faces reflected the light of a dozen fires. Pickup trucks were parked in rows, like coffins. Fists clutched pipes and chains.

Jarmaine said, "Did you see that?"

I nodded sadly. "I'm afraid so."

"Not down there," she said, pointing. "Over there."

On the horizon, lights winked. They started out tiny, like a swarm of lightning bugs, but soon sorted themselves into columns, two of them, stretching back toward downtown. They were federal marshals, and they had been sent by Robert Kennedy to save us. When the vehicles drew near, they came into view beneath the streetlights.

Jarmaine watched them. "Mail trucks?"

Stepping closer to the window, she gripped the wire mesh, then pounded the bricks angrily. "Mail trucks? Mail trucks!"

I wanted to speak but was afraid I might laugh or sob. I had expected the marshals to arrive in jeeps, maybe tanks, but not this. What were they going to do? Sort envelopes? Sell stamps?

The first group of mail trucks reached the park across Ripley Street, and the men got out. They didn't have uniforms. They wore work pants, open shirts, jackets, and yellow armbands saying *Marshal*.

Jarmaine stared at them. "They're good old boys."

Good old boys. It was an expression I'd heard my whole life. Good old boys were men who smiled and said hi and seemed harmless. I'd seen them my whole life—hanging around town, visiting at the hardware store, shaking hands and slapping each other on the back. I knew them as well as I knew myself. They might as well be uncles. Some of them were. As far as I was concerned, "good" meant good. Jarmaine felt otherwise.

As the other mail trucks arrived, they pulled in behind the first group, blocking them in.

Jarmaine shook her head. "They don't even know how to park."

The marshals got out, stumbling toward us with no apparent plan. A few of them recognized friends in the mob and stopped to say hello. Then they headed to Ripley Street in front of the church. Once there, they formed a rough line, like something a kindergartner might draw with a crayon. They looked at each other and waited.

About that time their leader, a man in a coat and tie, came running and shouting orders to them. "Disperse the crowd! Disperse the crowd!"

The marshals looked at each other, and a few of them pulled out objects that looked like beer cans.

I gaped. "They're going to drink?"

"That's not beer," said Jarmaine. "It's tear gas."

The marshals flipped something on the cans, then threw or rolled them into the crowd. It would have been a great idea, except for one thing—the wind.

Yellow-green gas billowed out of the cans, like smoke from a dragon. Instead of floating toward the crowd, it blew backward, carried by a breeze. The marshals coughed and sputtered, flapping their arms and trying desperately to wave away the gas.

"I can't see!" one of them screamed.

Panic set in. They stumbled, bumped into each other, and tried to grope their way back toward the trucks.

The marshals had been ordered to disperse the crowd. Wrong crowd.

But that wasn't the worst of it. The clouds of gas kept moving—past Ripley Street, past the marshals, and toward the church.

CHAPTER
THIRTY-TWO

The clouds settled around the front of the church, like an evil fog in a science-fiction movie.

Jarmaine said, "Do you smell it?"

I sniffed. "Not yet. Maybe we're above it."

The sanctuary wasn't. Its doors and windows were shut tight, but some of the gas must have seeped in, because a few moments later we heard a little boy's voice far below.

"Daddy, my eyes burn."

Other children cried, and people began to shout. Through it all, Gus played—first more hymns, then a song that caused people to stop and sing along. Their voices rose over the noise and confusion: "We shall overcome…"

A series of explosions rocked the building. Instinctively I ducked, but Jarmaine pulled me back up and pointed out the window.

"Look!"

A small group of teenagers had gathered in a corner of the park and was setting off firecrackers. They laughed. One of them grabbed a sparkler and ran through the crowd, waving it like a flag.

Jarmaine stared. "They think it's a party."

A marshal retreated past the boys, coughing, and I saw that he wasn't the only one. All the marshals were on the run. I wondered what Robert Kennedy would think.

The mob surged toward the church again, whooping and yelling. In the street, a man lit another rag in a bottle and tossed it up in our direction. We watched helplessly as it hit the roof below us and exploded, then slid off like an orange waterfall.

Just then I noticed someone else in the crowd, moving from group to group, observing and taking notes on a pad. It was Mr. McCall.

Next to him something flashed. I squinted in the darkness and made out a tall figure holding a camera.

"Grant!" I shouted. "Grant, I'm here!"

He had made it after all. Through the noise, though, he couldn't hear me.

I watched Grant and his father thread their way through the crowd, snapping pictures and taking notes. They passed a group of men who were sawing up planks and handing them out. Free weapon. Come and get it.

Standing near the group was someone I knew. He played horseshoes and listened to Alabama football games on the radio. He loved cornbread and black-eyed peas and was a good old boy. He liked to tell jokes and stories. I'd heard most of them, on fishing trips or when he tucked me in bed at night.

"Oh no," I moaned.

"What?" asked Jarmaine.

I couldn't bring myself to tell her. I watched as Daddy strode along the sidewalk, close enough to see but living in another world where white and black people didn't mix.

I had tried to leave home, but home had followed me.

I was white and always would be. I had never thought much about it until I'd met Jarmaine. She thought about the color of her skin every day. It made her who she was. Maybe my skin made me who I was, and I couldn't change it.

I studied Jarmaine's face. It was beautiful, not for its color or features, but because of who she was. You could read it in her eyes and see it in the firm line of her mouth. She was strong. I wanted to be strong too.

I watched Daddy, and my heart sank. My throat tightened. He stepped off the curb and spoke to someone. It was Mama, who held the baby in her arms.

Daddy lowered his head to hear her over the crowd. He nodded, and the two of them glanced around, scanning the scene. I noticed that he looked scared. So did she.

That's when it hit me. Daddy hadn't come to take part or even to watch. He had come for me.

I turned to Jarmaine, suddenly breathless. "It's my parents." I jumped and waved. "Mama! Daddy! Up here!"

Mama's head jerked upward, and she stared. She grabbed Daddy's arm and pointed to the tower.

Jarmaine, standing next to me, cried out. "Mother! It's my mother!"

Sure enough, Lavender stood next to my parents. I noticed that Daddy stayed close to her, protecting her from the mob.

I watched Lavender and saw that this time her face wasn't blank. It was twisted with fear as she searched for her daughter. Mama touched her shoulder and said something. Looking up, Lavender saw Jarmaine calling to her. Lavender stretched out her arms and beamed.

If I had ever wondered who she loved more, there was my answer.

Next to me, Jarmaine purred like a kitten.

I grabbed Jarmaine's arm and pulled her toward the ladder. I had to reach my parents and let them know I was fine.

"Come on!" I said.

Jarmaine followed me out of the tower and through the attic. We pounded down the stairs, past the door to the balcony, and on toward the first floor. I noticed a faint odor and my eyes stung, but we kept going.

At the bottom of the stairs, we found Reverend Abernathy talking urgently with Dr. King, James Farmer, and Diane Nash. They had cleared out the narthex, and I could see why. Fists pounded the outside of the big front doors, causing them to jump and shake. Below the doors, gas seeped in.

Jarmaine tried to hold me back, but I shook free and went running up to tell them about my parents. As I began to speak, Dr. King shot me a look. His eyes flashed. It was like seeing the face of God.

My words died in my throat. I huddled with Jarmaine as Dr. King turned back to the others.

He said, "It's bad out there. The marshals didn't help."

Reverend Abernathy nodded grimly. "The crowd wants blood."

Dr. King was thoughtful for a moment. "Maybe we should give it to them."

"How?" asked Farmer.

"We're the ones they want," said Dr. King. "If we surrender to the crowd, we might save the people."

His gaze was like steel. The others met it and didn't look away.

I tried to picture what the crowd would do if Dr. King and the others stepped outside. It was too terrible to imagine.

Reverend Abernathy shook his head. "No one's going out there," he said softly. "And we won't surrender— we'll negotiate. We'll go to my office, call Washington, and tell them what we need."

Farmer eyed Dr. King. King looked at Diane Nash, the student who had made out her will just a few days before. She nodded, and so did he.

Reverend Abernathy got several big, burly men to guard the doors. Then he headed downstairs, followed by Diane Nash, James Farmer, and Dr. King.

I watched the men at the door, then turned to Jarmaine. "Now what do we do?"

"I guess we wait," she said.

We wouldn't be the only ones waiting. Our parents, certain now that we were in the church, would be eager to see us.

We climbed back to the tower. I shut the trapdoor behind us, then went to a window and gazed out. Jarmaine came and stood next to me. We spotted our parents again and waved. If there was trouble, I was hoping they would be all right.

After a while, Jarmaine said, "You asked what we'll do next. What about after tonight? What are you planning to do?"

Jarmaine was my friend. Considering what we'd been through together, I owed her the truth. But what was the truth? My parents were prejudiced, and so was I. We loved each other and didn't always love others. We felt uncomfortable around people who were different. Sometimes we hurt them, even if it was just by watching.

What was I planning to do?

Get on the bus. Change. Stop watching and do something. Through it all, keep dreaming.

In my travels with Jarmaine, I had learned something about dreams. They aren't misty, sparkly things. They're roads to the future, like the road we had traveled in the Greyhound bus. There are twists and turns. You can't always see what comes next.

I shrugged. "I wish I knew."

"You're helping," said Jarmaine.

I thought of the way Dr. King and the others down-stairs had looked at me.

"Am I?" I asked. "Maybe I don't belong here."

"You belong," said Jarmaine. "You're my friend."

I don't know why, but I thought of a contest at our church picnic. Couples would stand next to each other, tie their legs together, and try to run. It was called a three-legged race. I had entered once with Daddy, and when we took off across the grass, we went laughing and tumbling to the ground.

Jarmaine and I barely knew each other, but some-how we were bound together. Black and white, we were in a three-legged race next to the Freedom Riders. We were lurching along, all of us, trying not to fall.

There was a noise in the attic below us. We heard footsteps, and they grew louder by the moment. People were charging up the steps. Maybe the mob had broken down the door. Maybe they were coming to get us. I shrank back, looking for a place to hide. The trapdoor flew open, and men came bursting through.

They weren't white. They were black, and there were five of them. They had coats and ties, and some-thing else: guns.

When the first man saw us, he stopped short and the others bumped into him, tipping like bowling pins. If we had been anywhere else it might have been funny.

Jarmaine stepped forward. "What are you doing?" she asked.

The leader glanced around, as if looking for help. The man behind him pointed outside, where flames burst and flickered. With his other hand he waved a pistol. It glinted in the dim light.

"We're fighting back."

I gaped at him. "You're going to shoot at them?"

A third man nodded. "Let's see how they like it."

"This is a church!" said Jarmaine. "You brought guns to church?"

"We thought there might be trouble," said the leader. "We were right."

He moved to a window and looked out. "This is the perfect spot," he said.

Jarmaine pleaded, "Don't fight violence with violence."

"They started it," the leader replied.

He lifted his foot and kicked the wire mesh, tearing it loose from the window. The others spread out around the tower and did the same.

I'd been watching, frozen. Our parents were out

there. So were Grant and Mr. McCall. What if the men shot them?

I tried to imagine what the mob would do if anyone got hurt or killed. I pictured them charging the church doors, splintering them and pouring inside where people were huddled.

The men raised their weapons.

"Don't do it!" cried Jarmaine. "Do you want to be like them?"

She threw herself at one of the men, knocking him sideways, but the others didn't even pause. Maybe I could stop one, but it wouldn't be enough. Five against two, and the five were armed.

In that instant I thought of what I had learned from Jarmaine. I recalled the courage of Dr. King. I thought of Gus and the power of music.

I remembered the bell.

Diving toward the center of the tower, I reached past the railing for the rope. I felt its rough fibers in my hands. I gripped it hard and pulled.

CHAPTER THIRTY-THREE

The bell swung, and the tower came alive.

I had heard the sound before, but this was different. Now, like the people at First Baptist Church, I needed it.

The sound was beautiful. It was strong. It was big and round, like a globe, like the earth. It shook the tower, and it shook me.

The men hesitated. They stared at the bell, their faces full of shock and wonder.

I rang the bell for all the people who had worked to bring it there and had cared for it faithfully. I rang it for Jarmaine and Lavender and Diane Nash. I rang it for Grant and Mr. McCall, for Mama and Daddy and all the other people who had been wrong and could change, if only they would try. I rang it for me.

I pulled the rope over and over again, filling the tower. The leader watched, then turned back toward the window. So did the others. When they did, they saw a row of flashing lights.

Jarmaine climbed to her feet. The two of us moved up beside the men and looked outside.

"Soldiers!" exclaimed Jarmaine.

Later we learned what had happened. Dr. King had called Washington and told Robert Kennedy that the marshals hadn't helped. When Kennedy considered using federal troops, Governor Patterson decided to act first, sending in the Alabama National Guard. They were escorted by the Montgomery police, whose flashing lights had appeared as if summoned by the bell.

I turned to the men in the windows. "You don't need your guns."

They looked at each other, then lowered their weapons and put them away.

Jarmaine grinned and shouted, "Thank you, Dr. King!"

The bell was silent, but inside me it kept on ringing.

* * *

We climbed from the tower and raced down the stairs, just behind the men who had burst in on us a few minutes before. The men seemed excited, but now it was a good excitement, and there was no sign of guns.

When we passed the big front doors, I saw the guards standing there. I hurried up to one of them, who was wearing a suit and drenched in sweat.

"Can I go outside?" I asked.

He gave me a funny look.

"It's okay," I added quickly. "I have friends there."

He said, "Nobody's going outside yet. It's too risky. The National Guard's mopping up."

Jarmaine took my hand and pulled me toward the sanctuary. I resisted for a moment, thinking of my parents, then realized it wouldn't do them any good if I got hurt.

We went into the sanctuary and made our way to the front, where we reclaimed our seats behind Gus. She finished a hymn and leaned down to us, beaming.

"I heard the news. Isn't it wonderful?"

There was a commotion at the back of the room. Dr. King, Reverend Abernathy, James Farmer, and Diane Nash were coming down the aisle, touching hands that were extended toward them. When they finally reached the front, Dr. King mounted the pulpit.

"Praise the Lord!" he shouted in a voice like a foghorn, and the crowd shouted back.

He told us that the governor had declared a state of martial law. The National Guard had been called out, and they were stationed outside the church.

The crowd roared.

Dr. King leaned in close to the microphone. "Brothers and sisters, I tell you that the law may not be able to make a man love me. But, by God, the law can keep him from lynching me."

The crowd erupted again.

Dr. King spoke about freedom and hope and the state of Alabama. When he finished, Reverend Abernathy came forward, then James Farmer took his place. There must have been a dozen preachers, and all of them preached. Afterward Gus made music, and the people joined in. By the time the meeting ended, it was midnight.

That should have been the end of it, but there was more.

I wanted to see my parents and Grant. Jarmaine went with me and we tried to leave, only to find that the National Guard wouldn't let us out.

"Sorry," said a young soldier stationed at the front door. "Protective custody."

Jarmaine demanded, "Protection from what? The mob's heading home."

The soldier shook his head. "I have orders."

There were voices behind us. When I turned around, Dr. King stood there.

"I'm going outside," he told the soldier.

"Sir—"

The young man moved to block the door, but Dr. King brushed him away and strode down the front steps. I tried to squeeze in behind, but the soldier grabbed my arm. As he did, I looked past him at the scene in front of the church.

At the bottom of the steps, Dr. King huddled with a tall, red-faced man who wore a helmet and a shoulder full of stripes. Beyond them, a ring of National Guardsmen with rifles held back the dwindling crowd. In the crowd were Grant and Mr. McCall. Daddy, Mama, and Lavender were next to them.

It was just a glimpse, but it was enough. They were there, waiting for us.

CHAPTER THIRTY-FOUR

The soldier pushed me back inside, where I found myself next to Jarmaine and a growing crowd, including Reverend Abernathy. A moment later the doors opened, and Dr. King came back in. Behind him was the soldier he had been speaking with outside.

Dr. King turned to Reverend Abernathy. "Ralph, this is General Graham. He showed me the governor's declaration. I've asked him to read it to the people."

Nodding curtly to Reverend Abernathy, Graham followed Dr. King into the sanctuary. We tagged along to see what would happen, settling into our familiar spot behind Gus. She looked exhausted but kept playing anyway. According to my reckoning, she'd been at it for nine hours.

Dr. King led General Graham to the pulpit and motioned for Gus to stop. Graham unfolded a sheet of paper. The crowd leaned forward, waiting to hear the news of their release.

The general put on a pair of glasses and cleared his throat. "Whereas, as a result of outside agitators coming into Alabama to violate our laws and customs…"

Cries rang out as Graham continued. I thought of Diane Nash and the students. It was hard to think of them as outside agitators.

Graham, reading on, raised his voice so he could be heard. The declaration said that the federal government "…by its actions encouraged these agitators to come into Alabama to foment disorders and breaches of the peace."

Someone called out, "We didn't breach the peace. They did!"

"Amen!" someone shouted.

Graham finished reading, then folded up the paper and put it into his pocket. "Folks, I didn't write it. I just enforce it. Now, I'm afraid you'll have to stay here a while longer. Get comfortable, because it looks like you'll be spending the night at church."

There was a loud chorus of boos. I doubted that anyone had been booed in the church before, unless maybe it was Satan.

Graham set his jaw, and Dr. King led him back up the aisle. A moment later they were gone.

Muttering, the people settled in for the night. Some of them tried to sleep. It wasn't easy, because the pews were crowded, the sanctuary was sweltering, and the smell of tear gas hung over the place. Someone got the idea of taking the children to the basement where there was a cool floor and more room.

Dr. King disappeared into the church office for a while and finally came out, relinquishing the phone to a line of people who wanted to call home. Afterward he circulated through the church, encouraging the people and offering kind words. Through it all, Gus played—hymns of encouragement, then quiet chords and softer songs, music to sleep by.

During one of the songs I slid in next to Gus on the organ bench. "Are you all right? You look so tired."

She smiled at me, her fingers never leaving the keys. "Honey, I'm past tired. I'm in another place. It's beautiful, isn't it?"

I looked up at the organ pipes and stained-glass window. The church certainly was beautiful, but I had a feeling that it wasn't the place Gus had in mind.

When I got up from the organ I didn't see Jarmaine. Then I looked down and spotted her sleeping under the bench, clutching a hymnal to her chest. I made my way around her, slipped off into the narthex, and climbed the stairs to the attic and the ladder to the tower. I closed the trapdoor behind me, then moved to a window overlooking Ripley Street.

The moon was rising in the west—half-white, half-black, not so different from the world I was learning to live in. Below, the National Guard was spread out along the front of the church, rifles ready, helmets glinting in the moonlight. Some of the crowd was gone, leaving a smaller group gathered outside the line of guardsmen.

I spotted Lavender and my parents, with Mr. McCall next to them. Grant handed them bottles of Coke and took a sip from his own as I watched. When he tilted his head, I waved.

"Grant!" I yelled. "Up here!"

Lowering the bottle, he stared, then pointed and excitedly told the others. They called to me, but I couldn't hear what they were saying. Watching their lips, though, I could make out one word. Through all the confusion, Daddy mouthed it: *Billie, Billie, Billie,* over and over again like a silent kiss.

I stayed there most of the night. I didn't sleep. I just wanted to see my parents and let them see me.

The air was still. The night was hot. The moon,

climbing in the sky, turned pink and orange. As the sun rose, a convoy of jeeps and trucks drove up Ripley Street. The first driver got out and spoke with General Graham, who nodded and barked out orders to a nearby soldier. The soldier hurried up the steps and threw the church doors wide open, the way they were meant to be.

The long night was over.

CHAPTER THIRTY-FIVE

I hurried down to the open doors, where I watched the people streamed outside, like water over a dam. They laughed and cried and praised God, breathing in fresh air and tasting a kind of freedom.

Jarmaine, wide-awake now, was among them. I watched from the doorway as she ran down the steps. Lavender, waiting at the bottom, gave her a fierce hug, then grabbed her and shook her. I remembered that shake. It was no fun.

I hurried down after her, looking for my parents. Before my foot hit the street, something hit me. It was big and lanky, and there was a camera dangling around its neck.

"Billie! You're all right!"

Grant wrapped his arms around me and squeezed. I squeezed back, thinking of Forsyth's Grocery, baseball cards, Top 40 records, and the long road I had traveled.

I stepped away and looked up at Grant. "Get any good pictures?"

"A few. My dad let me come. He said it might be dangerous, but it was important."

Mr. McCall stood nearby. "We're glad you're safe," he told me.

Mama came running. "Oh, Billie."

She threw herself at me and hugged so hard that it could have been a greeting or a punishment. Maybe it was a little of both.

She held me at arm's length. "Never ever run off again, you hear?"

I wasn't sure I could agree to that. I did know I was happy to see her.

Beyond her, holding the baby, stood Daddy. His eyes were red and puffy. He looked me up and down, drinking me in the way he had gulped a Coke the night before. I had always thought of him as strong, but that morning he looked small and sad.

"We were worried," he said. "We didn't know where you'd gone. Then Grant spotted you on that bus. He told us about the meeting in Montgomery, and we decided to follow you."

Mama added, "I called Lavender to watch the baby. She said Jarmaine was gone too."

"I told them you and Jarmaine were friends," said Grant. "We figured you must have gone together. Yesterday afternoon we drove to Montgomery in two cars. Lavender came with us."

"Why did you leave?" Daddy asked me, almost pleading.

"I was tired of watching. I wanted to do something."

Someone touched my arm. I looked around and saw Jarmaine with Lavender beside her.

I noticed Mama and Daddy staring at Jarmaine, and I realized the only time they had ever seen her was at the spelling bee, a thousand years ago. Lavender had cooked my meals and held me when I was sick, and they had never even met her daughter.

"This is Jarmaine Jones," I told them. "She's my friend."

"Jarmaine is an intern at the *Star*," said Mr. McCall. "She helps me with research." He turned to Jarmaine. "I hope you took good notes. We have a story to write."

"We saw the Freedom Riders," I said.

Daddy sighed.

I turned to him and said, "We saw their leader. Her name is Diane Nash. You know what? You'd like her."

"Lord help us," said Mama.

Daddy shook his head. "Those people are trouble."

Lavender shot him a look I'd never seen before, proud and angry at the same time. It occurred to me that this was a different person from the one who worked at our house.

"Those people are heroes," she said. "The world is changing, Mr. Sims. You'd best get used to it."

He stared at her. After all those years, they were meeting for the first time. I wondered if the real Lavender would disappear again behind the mask. I hoped she wouldn't.

The world was changing. I was changing. Maybe Daddy could too. It wouldn't have to be a big change— just a little adjustment here and there. He might give Lavender a day off. Maybe he would let her park in the driveway. A thousand little changes—in my neighborhood, across my town, around my country—might equal a big change.

Mama, who had been studying me, took the baby from Daddy. "I'm tired. Let's go."

"Not yet," I said, glancing at Jarmaine. "There's one more thing we need to do."

Jarmaine nodded, and the two of us climbed the front steps of the church. The bricks, glowing in the sunrise, seemed redder than ever. We moved through the crowd and into the sanctuary, which was nearly empty. Light filtered through the stained-glass window, throwing colors onto the church wall.

Among the colors, at the front of the room, Gus gathered up her music.

"Hey," I said to her.

Gus looked around and saw us. "Hello, my dears."

"How long did you play?" I asked.

She checked her watch. "Fifteen hours, give or take forever."

"Did you reach that place you were going?"

"Honey, I live in that place."

Jarmaine leaned over and, ever so gently, kissed Gus on the forehead.

"You are a rock," Jarmaine told her.

Gus closed her eyes, as if enjoying a cool breeze. "I'm a very small rock. Maybe a pebble."

"I rang the bell," I told her proudly.

"Feels good, doesn't it?"

I flexed my fingers, remembering the roughness of the rope and the sound of the chime. I told her, "Thank you for helping us. Thank you for showing us the tower.

Thank you for the bell."

Gus said, "That old bell doesn't need help from me. It speaks for itself. You listened, that's all."

Jarmaine picked up her basket, and we left First Baptist Church for the last time. Outside, our parents were waiting in an awkward group. The baby yawned, and I did too.

Mama chuckled. "Now it's time to go."

"Hey," said Grant, "we need a picture."

He lined us up—Daddy and Mama with the baby, Lavender with Mr. McCall, Jarmaine and me in front. Behind us the church stood tall, its tower pointing toward heaven.

"Okay, smile," said Grant. "At least, don't fall asleep."

The camera flashed, and we turned to leave. We walked up Ripley Street, past worshipers and news reporters. In the dim morning light, it was hard to tell who was black or white. I wished the world were like that.

CHAPTER THIRTY-SIX

Believe it or not, I went to school that day. Word had spread about my trip to Montgomery, and people in the hallways had some things to say. I ignored them. I was too tired to listen.

That afternoon, I sat on the front porch waiting for Arthur the Arm, and he showed up right on time. Giving the paper a neat twirl, he tossed it at my feet. I waved my thanks and opened it up.

Capitol Quiet, Tense

MONTGOMERY – Downtown Montgomery is quiet today—but it is an uneasy quiet, and there is a strong feeling of tension in the air.

There is no crowd at all around a Negro church where bloody rioting broke out last night, resulting in a proclamation of martial law by Gov. John Patterson.

The story went on to describe the events of the long night. Mr. McCall had been as good as his word, because at the top of the story were two names: Tom McCall and Jarmaine Jones. Beside it were Grant's photos. Seeing the pictures was like being there— hearing the crowd and ringing the bell.

"Want to toss the football?"

I looked up and saw Daddy, back from work early. He had loosened his tie and slung his coat over one shoulder. I tried to measure his mood but couldn't.

"Okay," I said.

He dropped his coat on the swing and fetched the ball.

"Go long," he said.

I dropped the paper and headed across the yard, running fast, the way Daddy had taught me. He waited, then sent the ball spinning in a long arc, over my shoulder and into my arms. Then he jogged across the front of the house, and I hit him with a spiral.

Later, we sat on the porch steps and drank some iced

tea. I'd been thinking all afternoon about what to say. When I opened my mouth, it spilled out.

"Here's the thing," I said. "Jarmaine's smart. She's strong. You should talk to her sometime."

He sipped his tea and gazed out across the yard.

I said, "Her mother helped raise me, but you never set foot in her house. Don't you think that's strange?"

He took another sip of tea.

"You watched the bus burn and didn't do a thing," I said.

He eyed me for a minute, then looked away. Mrs. Wilson, a neighbor, walked down the street with her dog, Buster, on a leash. She waved, and Daddy waved back.

"That's true," he said.

"I watched too. It was wrong."

"Some people in town would disagree," said Daddy.

"They're crackers," I said.

His head swiveled around, and he stared at me. "Where did you hear that word?"

"Different places."

"Am I a cracker?" he asked.

"You're my father. You're good. Aren't you?"

"You tell me. You're the expert. You run away from home, and you come back talking like this."

I set my iced tea on the porch. "That day at Forsyth's Grocery, people did terrible things. You watched, and so did I. That makes us part of it."

He sighed and shook his head. There were lines around his eyes and mouth. Suddenly he looked older.

"We were wrong," he said. "But they were wrong too."

"The Freedom Riders?"

"So-called," he said.

"Daddy, they just wanted to ride the bus."

"They knew what would happen, and they came anyway. Of course they got hurt. When you stir up a hornet's nest, you get stung."

I picked up my iced tea and took a gulp. I wanted it to make me strong.

"I'm a Freedom Rider," I said.

I told him what Jarmaine and I had done on the bus and at the Birmingham Greyhound station. I expected him to be angry, but he surprised me.

"Oh, sweetheart," he said.

When I was six, I decided one day that I would climb the big tree in our front yard. I shinnied up the trunk, edged out onto one of the big branches, and stood. It was beautiful up there. Then Daddy saw me and came running out of the house. The look on his face that day was the look I saw now.

"You could have been hurt," he said.

"Maybe. It seemed like the right thing to do."

"Look, Billie, I don't know what you think or what you did. Just be careful. I need you safe."

"You love me," I said.

"Of course I do."

"Like Lavender loves Jarmaine."

"Yes," he said.

"Jarmaine doesn't believe in safe. She wants freedom."

Daddy shrugged. "Don't we all."

Maybe that was how it worked. You see things happen. You watch. You shrug. Then you move on. It seemed hopeless. But the Freedom Riders disagreed.

"Why are we like this?" I asked.

"Like what?"

"Scared of Negroes."

"That's crazy."

"We hold them down. We build separate schools. We send them to the back of the bus. What are we afraid of?"

He shook his head. "What did they tell you in that church?"

"Answer my question."

He shot me a look. The last time I had talked back

to him, he'd given me a whack and sent me to my room. This time he just watched me.

"Black and white don't mix," he said. "Around here, they never have."

"Why?"

"I don't know. Tradition. Culture. A way of life."

I said, "Tradition is Mama's corn pudding. This is more than that. People suffer. You saw that mob at the church. Someone could have been killed."

"It's the way things are."

"That's not good enough."

"What do you want me to say, Billie? It's wrong to have slaves. It's horrible. It's evil. But we did it. Haven't you ever done something you were ashamed of? You hide it, you push it down, and pretty soon it becomes part of you, like your arm or leg."

I tried to think of what Jarmaine would say.

"Cut it off," I told him.

"You have the answers, don't you? Cut it off. Repeal the law. Run away from home. Why did you leave?"

"I had to."

"I was worried," he said.

"I met Dr. King. I talked to a woman named Gus. They're just people."

"Don't run away," he said. "I want you safe."

"It's not about me."

But I was wrong. I saw it in his eyes and the hunch of his shoulders. He wanted to keep the world the way it was. For me. For Mama. The thing he was afraid of was the thing I dreamed of.

Change.

It was a road, and I wanted to take it. It scared me, but that was okay. I would change, and someday maybe Daddy would. Maybe the others would too.

A mosquito buzzed in my ear. Crickets chirped in the distance. I slipped my hand into Daddy's, and we sipped our iced tea.

* * *

After supper I went to Grant's house. His photos had run in the afternoon paper but there must have been more, because he was in his darkroom, working. Mrs. McCall led me back there, and I knocked.

"Grant, it's me."

"Just a minute."

A moment later he opened the door and motioned me inside. Closing it behind me, he switched off the light, and the room turned red.

"Are you doing black and white?" I asked.

He nodded and turned back to his work.

Pinned across the wall in front of him were strings

with photos clipped to them. There was First Baptist Church. There was the mob. There was the overturned car, with people holding bats and bricks. There was the shot of us in front of the church—Mr. McCall and Lavender, Mama and Daddy, Jarmaine and me. In the dim red light, we appeared to be covered with blood.

I shivered. "What do you think about all that?"

He shrugged. "I think the world is a strange and beautiful place."

"Were you scared?"

"Maybe at first. Then I got busy."

I nodded. "It's what you were put on this earth to do."

"Huh?"

"Taking pictures. Showing people the truth. You're only thirteen, but you've already got your life's work."

He poured some chemicals into a tray. That's the thing about your life's work. When you're doing it, you're more or less oblivious to other people.

Looking around the room, I noticed a photo pinned to the wall. It seemed to be from another time. It was me, standing in front of the Anniston bus station.

The picture showed a girl with a determined grin. She didn't know where she was going or what her life's work would be. Wherever she went, she would try to do what was right. She would be hard on herself and learn to forgive others. She would welcome change. She would dream it, then build it.

Grant stood beside me, lost in his work, dreaming his own dreams, tongue sticking halfway out of his mouth. Watching him, I had a funny thought. Maybe he would build it with me.

In the darkroom, I could imagine anything I wanted. Hands touched. Images appeared, as if by magic. The world was developing right before my eyes.

If I thought about it, dreamed about it, worked on it, maybe I could get a picture I liked. The picture would show a better place—Anniston or Montgomery or a city in the sky. And I would be there.

AUTHOR'S NOTE

There were more famous events in the history of the civil rights movement, many of which took place in Alabama—Selma, the Montgomery bus boycott, the bombing of a Birmingham church. But in some ways it all began in Anniston, in a bus, in the lives of misguided people who, building on years of resentment and hate, did awful things while good people, like Billie and her father, stood by and watched.

Billie Sims, Jarmaine Jones, Grant McCall, and their families are fictional, but the events against which their story is told are true. On Mother's Day 1961, the Freedom Riders came to Anniston. An angry crowd surrounded their bus at the Greyhound station, then followed it to Forsyth & Son Grocery outside of town, where they terrorized the riders and burned the bus. It seemed that the only person who tried to help the riders was little Janie Forsyth, who just a week earlier had won the state spelling bee.

A few days later, those same victims were confronted and beaten at the Birmingham and Montgomery bus stations, the latter of which is now a museum dedicated to the Freedom Riders. The following Sunday, the riders attended a meeting at Montgomery's First Baptist Church, along with the church's pastor, Ralph Abernathy; Birmingham civil rights leader Fred Shuttlesworth; CORE's James Farmer; and Dr. Martin Luther King Jr. King spent much of the evening on the phone with Attorney General Robert Kennedy, trying to get the attention of an administration more interested in Moscow than Montgomery. Events in the story were taken from eyewitness accounts and film footage. A few church members really did bring guns but never used them.

I first learned of these events when I saw Stanley Nelson Jr.'s magnificent documentary *Freedom Riders*. I was riveted by the interview with Janie Forsyth McKinney, who recalled, "I went to the house and got a bucket of water and a stack of Dixie cups, and I walked right out into the middle of that crowd." Stunned by

Janie's bravery, I wondered what it would have been like to grow up in Anniston at that time and witness those events. It was the birth of Billie Sims.

Surprisingly little has been written about this important episode. The best book is Raymond Arsenault's *Freedom Riders: 1961 and the Struggle for Racial Justice*, which was later republished in an abridged version when the documentary film was shown on PBS's *American Experience*. Some of the Freedom Riders have written their own accounts, which give a more personal view.

One of the best sources of information is the *Anniston Star*, historically one of the South's outstanding newspapers. The day-by-day reporting described in this book is accurate and the articles quoted are real, though Tom McCall and his son, Grant, are fictional stand-ins for the heroic group of real-life reporters and photographers who covered the story.

As helpful as all these accounts were, the most inspiring was given to me by an elderly deacon at First Baptist Church one day in late February, when I had driven to Alabama to finish my research and see firsthand the places that would be in my story. I arrived at the church on a Saturday morning, hoping to snap a few pictures of the outside and, if I was lucky, to get a glimpse inside.

When I knocked on the back door, I was greeted by Benjamin E. Beasley, who, it turned out, was one of the church elders and saints. He and a few parishioners were busy mixing up pots of food for an event later that day, but he was generous enough to take nearly an hour and introduce me to his church, which he treated as an old friend.

He showed me the sanctuary with its stately organ pipes and stained-glass windows; the little office where Martin Luther King negotiated by phone with Robert Kennedy; and, most glorious of all, the tower and its beautiful old bell. He rang it for me, then told me proudly that his mother, Mildred Beasley, had been the organist that day at the Freedom Rider meeting, over fifty years earlier. She had started at three o'clock in the afternoon and had played off and on all night to inspire and comfort the congregation. I've tried to capture something of her spirit, as well as her son's, in the character of Gus.

I am grateful to Deacon Beasley, as well as to the librarians and researchers at the Anniston Public Library, the Freedom Rides Museum, the Alabama State Archives, and Vanderbilt University. I'm indebted to the students at Meigs Magnet School in Nashville, whose excitement when I told them about my Freedom Rider project was a constant source of inspiration.

Kristin Zelazko, my editor at Albert Whitman, caught the excitement and has been a champion for the book and for my writing ever since. Deepest gratitude to Kristin and the Albert Whitman team for their support and enthusiasm.

It was a special moment when Kristin put me in touch with Janie Forsyth McKinney, now living in Los Angeles and working at my alma mater, UCLA. Janie graciously read the manuscript, confirmed information about that terrible day and her part in it, and offered suggestions for a more accurate depiction of her father and his store. Meeting her has been an unexpected treat.

Heartfelt thanks go to my father and mother, Paul and Ida Sue Kidd, who grew up in the South and taught their children that all people deserve appreciation and respect, no matter what their race or ethnic origin.

And, as always, I'm most deeply grateful to my wife, Yvonne Martin Kidd, and my daughter, Maggie Kidd. They are my shining stars.

DISCUSSION QUESTIONS

1. Why do you think Billie was so fascinated by buses? What kind of bus ride did she dream of? How did it compare with the real bus ride she took with Jarmaine?

2. In Billie's town, it was not safe for African Americans to show all of their feelings. What feelings do you think Lavender and Jarmaine were hiding? Had they been able to express those feelings, what might they have said or done?

3. In the 1960s, some people did not treat African Americans well. What groups do we mistreat today? What could you personally do to change that?

4. Sometimes the people we love do things that hurt others. Sometimes we do things that hurt others. What did Billie learn about why we do this and how we can stop?

5. Billie experienced a different world when she went to Jarmaine's house and to the church rally. It was a world that existed alongside hers but had been invisible to her. Are there invisible worlds alongside yours? How might you enter them, and what might happen?

6. Why do you think it was important for Dr. King to come to the rally at the church? How did his actions influence events? How did his actions influence the people there?

7. What did it mean to Billie to ring the bell? How do you think she felt? Are there bells that you need to ring?

8. At the end of the story, Billie asked if Gus had reached the place she was going. Gus said, "Honey, I live in that place." What do you think Gus meant?

9. Billie, her family, and her friends were not real people, but the events in the story were real. What history did you learn from this story that you didn't know before? What else would you like to know about that time and place?

10. The characters in a story often change because of what happens to them. Did Billie and Jarmaine change, and if so, how? In what ways do you think they might act differently in the future because of their experiences?

11. Billie had been around Lavender all her life but didn't really know her. Are there people like that in your life? How could you get to know them better?

12. Janie Forsyth showed that you can be brave and be a leader even if you aren't an adult. What are some ways you could be brave and be a leader?

13. Billie admired Mr. McCall and thought she might like to do what he did. Who are some of the people you admire in your life? What have you learned from them?

14. Grant seemed sure of what to do with his life. Have you met people like that? Are you like that? If you met Grant, what would you ask him?

15. The events in the story were important moments in Billie's life that helped define her. What defining moments have you had in your life? What defining moments can you imagine in the future?

ABOUT THE
AUTHOR

Ronald Kidd is the author of more than ten novels for young readers, including the highly acclaimed *Monkey Town: The Summer of the Scopes Trial.* His novels of adventure, comedy, and mystery have received the Children's Choice Award, an Edgar Award nomination, and honors from the American Library Association, the International Reading Association, the Library of Congress, and the New York Public Library. He is a two-time O'Neill playwright who lives in Nashville, Tennessee.